An angel made her do it . . .

"Guess what?" Christina said. "I might take ballet lessons."

A bewildered expression crossed Ashley's lightly freckled face. "Ballet? I didn't know you wanted to study ballet."

Christina took Ashley's arm and spoke excitedly. "I've always wanted to, but I didn't get the chance when I was little. After that, I thought I was too old. But now I know it's still possible. I feel it. Really! I *need* to dance."

"You do?" Ashley asked doubtfully. "Why?"

"Because all of us—you, Katie, and me—we need to do special things now. We're not like regular people anymore."

"We're not?" Ashley asked, her pretty face twisting into a look of confusion.

"No, we're not," Christina said confidently, gazing steadily at Ashley with her sky-blue eyes. "We've been touched by angels."

Christina's Dancing Angel

FOREVER ANGELS

Christina's Dancing Angel

Suzanne Weyn

Published by Troll Associates, Inc. Rainbow Bridge is a trademark of Troll Associates.

Printed in the United States of America.

10 9 8 7 6 5 4 3 2 1

For Bob Bosworth, an earth angel

Christina's Dancing Angel

1

"It might already be too late," Christina said as she followed her mother into the stable. "But if I work hard, maybe I could catch up to the others. I mean, I really think I *could* catch up."

The horses stirred, shuffling in their stalls and neighing gently as Christina and her mother, Alice, entered the big, barnlike building.

Christina loved the heavy, damp air of the stable, thick with the pleasantly musky smell of horses. Usually she stopped to breathe it all in as soon as she entered. But today she was hardly aware of it. Her mind was on other more important things.

Her mother grabbed hold of a bale of hay and lugged it into an empty stall. With her pocket knife she deftly severed the cord binding the hay. "Why this sudden interest in ballet, Christina?" Alice asked at last.

Gathering her long, straw-colored hair into a ponytail, Christina scowled. She had to think a moment before she tried to explain. It wasn't easy to put into words. Her desire to study ballet came from a feeling—an impulse, a desire—and it was hard to describe. Something so . . . so insubstantial, so hard to put your finger on.

Besides that, Christina knew she had to pick her words carefully when she spoke to her mother about angels. It was a touchy subject.

"My wanting to study ballet isn't exactly sudden," she began as her mother pitchforked the fresh hay into the stall. "You know I've always liked ballet. I always watch whenever it's on TV."

"That's different from wanting to dance," her mother pointed out.

"Well, sure, it is," Christina agreed. She took a long, deep breath. How could she explain this without sounding nutty? "I've always sort of wanted to take ballet, but after a while I thought I was too old. Most girls start when they're six or seven. But now I'm not worried about that anymore. I want to try anyway."

"What made you change your mind?" Alice asked.

Christina took another deep breath. "It's because of angels," she said finally, deciding simply to tell the truth.

"Angels!" Abruptly, her mother stopped pitching hay. She stood straight and tall, shaking her blonde head sadly. "Oh, Christina," she said wearily, "not angels again. I was hoping you'd forgotten about all that."

Christina folded her arms defensively and pressed her lips into a hard line. She just couldn't stand the idea of having to have this conversation again for the millionth time.

Why wouldn't her mother believe her when she said she'd seen angels? It made Christina want to scream in frustration.

Her mother was usually so open-minded about things. She believed in the power of crystals to heal. She read tarot cards and tossed the I Ching. She even checked her horoscope every day. She'd always told Christina there were mysteries in life that simply couldn't be explained rationally.

So why wouldn't she believe Christina had seen angels?

Christina *had* seen them, and she wasn't going to be persuaded otherwise.

"Mom, angels are real," Christina insisted.

"That's not the point," her mother argued. "Whether angels are real or not, I find it hard to believe that you, Ashley, and Katie actually saw them."

"Why not?"

"People just don't go around seeing angels."

"*We* did," Christina said firmly.

Alice sighed and shook her head mournfully. "Maybe you should talk to a counselor at school," she said softly. "It couldn't hurt. Perhaps you think you saw angels because you *wish* you'd seen angels. A person's mind can play tricks. Are you having any problems you think you need angelic help to solve?"

Christina rolled her eyes and turned away from her mother in frustration. She didn't want to hear another word about seeing a counselor! Every time Christina tried to talk about angels, her mother brought this up.

"Okay, forget counseling," her mother said. "You can talk to *me* about anything that's bothering you, you know."

"I'm *okay*, Mom," Christina said sharply. "I'm not having any problems. There *are* angels in the woods. There are!"

"Christina," her mother sighed.

"You don't have to believe it if you don't want to," Christina said, feeling hopeless. She knew there was no point in continuing the conversation. They'd been through it before, and there was just no way she could convince her mother.

Alice gave Christina a long, searching look.

"I haven't seen the angels in awhile, anyway," Christina added. "I've just been thinking about angels, that's all."

Her mother's brows knit into a worried grimace.

"Not *all* the time," Christina amended. "I don't think about them all day long, or anything like that. But the other night, after you went to bed, I stayed up and watched TV. I was channel-surfing, and then I hit a ballet on some public television station. It was *Swan Lake*."

The memory of the ballet filled Christina with renewed excitement. She hung on the stall's chest-high door. "Mom, it was so beautiful," she said, remembering the wonderful flowing music and the gorgeous dancers dressed as swan maidens, gliding across the stage in feathered, billowing white costumes. "It was *so* beautiful it actually made me cry."

"It's such a sad story," her mother said, resuming her work.

"But Mom, that's not why I cried," Christina explained impatiently. "It was the way the dancers moved. The ballerinas were so light and graceful. It seemed that they couldn't possibly be human. When they leaped, they were more like angels. It was as if they had invisible wings that just lifted them into the air."

"That made you cry?" her mother asked, not unsympathetically.

Christina smiled sheepishly. "I know it sounds strange, but I just started crying. I'm not sure why, exactly."

It was true. She really didn't know why her eyes had filled with tears as she watched the ballet. She wasn't unhappy or sad about anything.

Everything was fine, really. She loved living at the ranch where her mother worked as a ranch hand and riding instructor. In fact, the Pine Manor Ranch was the best place she could possibly imagine living. The rolling pastures and surrounding pine forest were lovely. She could ride the horses whenever she wanted. Her best friend, Ashley, whose parents owned the ranch, lived right there, too.

Christina knew she was lucky to have a job working there this summer, too. Helping with the horses and trail rides was fun. So was working over at the bunk-house where the overnight guests stayed. Not many other eighth-graders she knew had managed to find summer jobs, except the ones who worked *their* parents' farms, which somehow wasn't the same.

No. Looking at it objectively, she knew things were fine. Yet inside herself, everything felt like it was moving, shifting around. Maybe it was because she was getting older, growing, changing.

Maybe it was because of her experience with the angels.

She didn't know. She *did* know that lately she'd felt a deep, inexplicable longing, as if her soul cried out for something she couldn't name.

Was that why she'd found herself weeping at *Swan Lake* there, alone, in the middle of the night? Because the beautiful ballet had answered her need?

"Maybe I cried because I felt so happy," she considered aloud. "People do that sometimes, don't they?" She herself had never cried out of happiness before, but perhaps that night had been the first time.

Her mother nodded thoughtfully. "Yes, people *do* sometimes cry when they feel moved by something. It can be something happy or something very beautiful. I cry sometimes when I feel very moved by a movie or a book."

"Moved," Christina said, rolling the word around on her tongue. "What does that mean, exactly?"

"It means that something touched your emotions," her mother said.

Christina stepped into the stall. "I guess that ballet moved me," she said. "I want to be able to do that, Mom. To dance like that must be the most wonderful thing on earth. I know thirteen is kind of old to start taking lessons, but I bet I could do it. I really want to try."

Perhaps her unnameable longing was a longing to dance, she'd wondered that night as the dancers' names scrolled across the screen at the end of the ballet.

"Where would you take lessons?" her mother asked.

"There's Amy's Academy of Dance," Christina told her. "You know, the place over the post office."

"How much does it cost?"

"I don't know, but I'll find out," Christina said eagerly. After all, her mother wouldn't ask what it cost if she weren't at least thinking about letting Christina do it.

"Find out and we'll *talk*," her mother said.

Impulsively Christina wrapped her mother in a hug and kissed her cheek. "Thank you! Thank you! Mom, you are the greatest!"

"I said we'll talk," her mother reminded her. "I'm not making any promises, okay?"

"I know, I know," Christina said happily. "But I just have this feeling. A real, *deep* feeling that I'm meant to do this. I'm meant to dance. I just know it."

"We'll see," her mother said, shaking her head in amused dismay. "In the meantime, run back to the house and get my work gloves, would you? I left them on the kitchen counter."

"Sure," Christina agreed. "Be right back."

Christina's sneakered feet were light as she hurried out of the stable. She leaped off the ground and punched the air. "Yes!" she cried.

She was going to take ballet lessons!

She hurried up the wide dirt path to the cabin where she and her mother lived. As she neared it, Christina caught sight of a petite girl with bouncy, shoulder-length red hair at the front door of the cabin.

A smile spread across Christina's face. "Ashley!" she called out, waving her arms in a greeting. She hurried toward her, anxious to tell her friend the news.

Ashley waved back, walking away from the door to meet up with Christina. "Hi," she said. "Want to go for a ride? Dad wants me to ride backup for a group he's taking out in about fifteen minutes."

"Okay," Christina agreed. "Guess what? I might take ballet lessons!"

A bewildered expression crossed Ashley's lightly freckled face. "Ballet? I didn't know you wanted to study ballet."

Christina took Ashley's arm and spoke excitedly. "I've always wanted to, but I didn't get the chance when I was little. After that, I thought I was too old. But now I know it's still possible. I feel it. Really. I *need* to dance."

"You do?" Ashley asked doubtfully. "Why?"

"Because all of us—you, Katie, and me—we need to do special things now. We're not like regular people anymore."

"We're not?" asked Ashley, her pretty face twisting into a look of confusion.

"No," Christina said confidently, gazing steadily at Ashley with her sky-blue eyes. "We've been touched by angels."

2

Unlike Christina's mother, Ashley believed in the angels. She'd seen them herself. Christina knew she could make Ashley understand.

"Don't you see?" Christina continued excitedly. "We've all had this incredible experience. Now we know there's more to life than just plain old humdrum living."

Spreading the fingers of one hand, Ashley studied her perfectly manicured nails. "I suppose," she replied slowly, as if she wasn't really sure. "But why does that make you think you have to be a dancer?"

"I've always liked to dance, and I've wanted to study ballet. And I realized last night that being a ballerina is the closest thing to being an angel. At least, for me it is."

Ashley folded her arms across her crisply ironed white cotton shirt. She squinted her green eyes. "I'm not following this. Do you mean you had some kind of mystical revelation about ballet?" she asked skeptically.

"No, it's not that, exactly," Christina told her. "It's just a feeling I have, an intuition. I can't explain it, but you know what I mean, don't you?" she appealed to her friend.

Ashley's expression relaxed, and she nodded. "Well, your feelings usually are pretty amazing," she said.

"They are, aren't they?" Christina agreed. Suddenly she felt embarrassed. "I know that sounds conceited."

"No, it doesn't," Ashley assured her. "A lot of the time you get those strange feelings, those intuitions of yours, you're right. I don't know why. Maybe you have ESP."

"I might," Christina said. She'd often suspected that she had some power she didn't fully understand. She couldn't predict earthquakes or elections or anything like that. But, in her own small way, she sometimes had a sense of how her day would unfold or what would happen to a friend.

"Come on inside with me," she told Ashley. "I have to bring Mom her work gloves. I want to change out of this workshirt, too. It's getting hot."

The moment they entered the cozy, rustic cabin, its cool air embraced them. With its beamed low ceiling and slate rock wall where the fireplace stood, the cabin never got too hot, even with the late July sun beating down. The simply furnished living room with its plain, prairie-style furniture, was only separated from the airy kitchen by a long wooden counter. Christina instantly spied her mother's worn brown leather gloves lying on top of it.

Ashley meanwhile had flopped onto the soft brown couch facing the stone fireplace. Leaning forward, she grabbed a large coffee-table book entitled *Healing with Herbs* and began thumbing through it. "Do you think this stuff really works?" she asked Christina, nodding toward the book.

"Sure. I mean, why not?" Christina replied. "Remember how Junior recovered when he ate the angelbloom flowers you found in the woods?"

Ashley nodded thoughtfully. "But Junior is a horse," she said.

"So? Same difference," Christina insisted.

"I guess," Ashley conceded as she began studying the book intently.

"I'll be right back, okay?" Christina called as she headed past the living room toward her small bedroom. Once there, she pulled off her denim shirt. She changed into what she called a T-cool, an extra-large man's white T-shirt. She'd carefully sewn Native American-style beads at its hem and used fabric paints to create a beadwork effect at the collar. It was one of her favorite shirts. Since today was turning out so well, she was in the mood to wear it.

She left on her jeans, since she'd be riding, but kicked off her sneakers. She didn't like to wear them riding because they made her feet slip in the stirrups.

Rummaging in her disorganized closet, she found a pair of tannish brown work books she'd bought recently. Their definite heel held her foot more firmly in the stirrup. *I guess that's why you always see cowboys wearing boots*, she mused.

She whipped her long hair out of the ponytail and raced a brush through it. Quickly, she wove it into two braids. It seemed more in keeping with her shirt that way.

When the braids were done, Christina studied the total effect in a mirror. It would look better if she had dark, glossy hair, with dark mysterious eyes to go with it. Christina had always wished she looked darkly exotic instead of fair-haired and stereotypically all-American. "You look more like Heidi than any kind of Indian," she muttered to her braided image. "Bor-ing," she sighed as she headed out of her room.

Stopping in the kitchen, she grabbed the gloves and stuffed them carelessly in a back pocket. Under the gloves she found that morning's *Pine Ridge Courier*. She quickly unfolded the newspaper to check the horoscope section.

"What does mine say?" Ashley asked, looking up from *Healing with Herbs*.

"Libra. Now is a perfect time to save money," Christina read, leaning against the counter. "Avoid rash purchases. Invest wisely."

Ashley put down the book and frowned. "Mine always says boring stuff like that," she complained. "I hate that. Who knows if it's even true? I only look at my horoscope when I'm with you. You make it seem like it could actually be for real."

"It *is* for real," Christina insisted. "Listen to what

mine says! 'Aquarius. Everything has been leading to this moment. Follow your instincts.' "

She put down the paper and stared wide-eyed at Ashley. "Can you believe that?" she asked.

"It must mean Matt," Ashley said excitedly. "He's going to ask you out. That's got to be it!"

Matt Larson was a boy in their class, and Christina had a huge crush on him. He'd never asked Christina out before, and now that it was summer, Christina only ran into him occasionally around town or at the mall.

"That would be very cool," Christina considered. "But I don't think that's what the horoscope means. When I read this, the first thing I thought of was ballet. Everything has been leading up to my taking ballet lessons."

"Do you really think so?" Ashley asked doubtfully.

"Sure," Christina insisted.

"Ballet lessons *and* going out with Matt," Ashley offered as an optimistic compromise.

"Okay. And Matt, too," Christina agreed. She smiled at her friend. That was Ashley, all right, the diplomatic one, always looking for an answer that made everyone happy.

And maybe Ashley was right about ballet *and* Matt. Why not? Christina was suddenly feeling lucky, amazingly in tune with all the mysterious forces of the universe.

Spreading her arms wide, she closed her eyes and whirled around the room in a wildly exaggerated ballet.

Leaping in the air, she landed gracefully in a curtsy in front of Ashley.

"Come on," Ashley said, giggling. "We have to help my dad with the trail ride, and your mom is waiting for those gloves."

"Oh, right," said Christina, comically collapsing her tall frame to the floor. "I almost forgot."

Scrambling to her feet, Christina headed out the front door with Ashley behind her. They were on the dirt road leading to the stable when Ashley grabbed hold of Christina's arm.

"What?" Christina asked.

"Look who's there," Ashley said, wrinkling her nose in distaste.

Shielding her eyes from the sun, Christina peered down the road toward the front of the stable where Ashley's father was getting a group ready to go out on a trail ride. One striking figure stood out from the others; a tall, slim girl in tan riding boots, a sleeveless white T-shirt, and crisp white summer pants. A colorful Navajo belt adorned her delicate waist. From beneath a stylish Stetson hat, one perfect white-blonde braid trailed down her back.

"It's our favorite person," Ashley muttered sarcastically.

"I know," Christina moaned. Her wonderful mood began to ebb away fast.

3

As Ashley and Christina stared glumly down the road, the thunderous roar of a motorcycle shattered the quiet behind them.

Christina turned away from the stable to look. A black and chrome motorcycle was kicking up a small dust storm as it approached on the dry dirt road.

The bike stopped several feet away, and its driver waited impassively while his passenger climbed off. As she pulled off her helmet, a burst of wildly electric auburn hair swung around her shoulders. She strapped the helmet to the back of the bike, and the driver zoomed off without even waving good-bye.

"I didn't know Katie was coming over, did you?" Ashley asked Christina. "Doesn't she have today off?"

Katie was the third member of their trio. This summer Ashley had talked her parents into giving Katie a job at the ranch, too. Most of the time she worked over at the old bunkhouse. After years of neglect, the bunkhouse recently had been renovated, reopened, and renamed the Pine Ranch Inn.

"I didn't *think* she was working," Ashley said, "but I guess she is."

Christina waved to Katie.

The tall, broad-shouldered girl spent a minute swatting dirt from the dusty road off her jeans and sleeveless denim shirt. Then she looked up, her face breaking into a dazzling smile, and waved back energetically.

"Hi, guys," she called brightly as she walked toward them. "Your mom called me this morning, Ashley. They're shorthanded at lunch, so she wants me to help serve. I had no way over, but Mel was riding this way, so I figured I'd ride with him and hang out until they need me."

"Cool," Christina said. "How much did it cost?" Katie's cousin Mel always charged her when he took her anywhere on his motorcycle. Katie's lively warm brown eyes sparkled happily. "Nothing," she reported gleefully.

"No way!" Christina laughed in disbelief.

"Way," Katie countered. "Mel's probably feeling guilty or something," she added.

"Maybe he's getting to like you," Christina suggested.

Katie snorted disdainfully. "Who can tell with Mel? All he does is grunt."

Christina noticed Ashley had gone back to peering

down the road. Katie noticed, too. "What are you gawking at?" she asked Ashley in her usual blunt manner.

"Look who's down by the stable," Ashley whispered.

Katie shielded her eyes against the sun and peered down the road. "Ew, yuck! Molly Morgan. What's she doing here?"

"Going on a trail ride, I suppose," Ashley flatly said.

"Oh, well, who cares?" Katie waved her hand dismissively.

The girls began walking down the road toward the stable. "You're right," Christina agreed. "Who cares?"

Molly Morgan was in their eighth-grade class at Pine Ridge Middle School. She was the captain of the cheerleaders and at the center of a really snobby group of kids.

"I told Dad I'd ride backup on this trail ride, but if Molly Morgan thinks I'm here to be her slave, she can just forget it," Ashley fumed.

"You *are* here to serve her," Katie pointed out bluntly.

Ashley glowered at Katie. "Not the way she looks at it."

"Forget about her," Katie said. "She's just a stuck-up little witch. The private school I used to go to was full of girls like her."

"You went to private school?" Christina gasped. Even though she'd known Katie for months now, there was so much she was still finding out about her.

"Sure," Katie said nonchalantly. "My mother taught English there, so I got to go there, too. Otherwise we probably couldn't have afforded it. It was full of *really* rich kids."

This was the first time Christina had heard Katie mention her mother without getting a distant, hurt expression in her eyes. Katie's parents had died in a car accident the previous year. Now Katie lived with her aunt and uncle and her cousin, Mel.

Losing her parents and suddenly moving from the city to rural Pine Ridge had been a huge adjustment for Katie. At first all her defenses had been high, and she'd approached everyone with a hard, tough-kid-from-the-city attitude. Ashley had somehow seen through the act and befriended Katie in spite of it. Then Christina got to know Katie because of Ashley. Now all three were close friends, maybe even closer than usual for best friends. But, after all, they'd shared an incredible, one-in-a-million experience.

"Your school was full of girls like *her*?" Ashley said incredulously. "How could you stand it? You, of all people!"

Katie shrugged. "A lot of them weren't *that* bad once you got to know them." Remembering, she smiled. "But some were even *worse* than you can imagine." She sighed. "There were some real monsters at that school. You just had to get to know them and learn who was horrible and who was nice."

"Yeah, like who could ever even get to know Molly Morgan?" Ashley muttered. "She's so stuck-up she won't even say hello."

"Forget about her," Katie advised. "Act like *she's* the one who's not there."

As the girls finally reached the riding group, Ashley's father, Mr. Kingsley, smiled at them. His pleasant, deeply lined face was shadowed by the brim of his baseball cap. "Saddle up fast, Ashley," he said. "We're just about ready to go."

On the spur of the moment, Ashley invited Katie to join them. "Want to ride?"

"I guess so," Katie said. "I still have another two hours to kill."

"Katie and Christina are coming, too," Ashley told her father.

"Katie, can you ride?" Mr. Kingsley asked her.

"A little," Katie told him honestly.

"She'll stay with Christina and me," Ashley assured him.

"All right," her father said agreeably. "But, remember, you girls can't all be gabbing together back there, Ashley. You have to look out for the other riders, too."

"No problem," Ashley said.

Christina turned to Katie and said, "Come on, let's get horses."

They followed Ashley toward the stable. On the way in, Christina glanced quickly at Molly. Already seated atop her white horse, she was studying her long, pale pink fingernails and looking bored.

Beside her, on a black horse, sat a thin woman with short, perfectly styled light blonde hair. Christina recognized her as Mrs. Morgan, Molly's mother.

Just as Christina was passing Molly, she looked down at her, a spark of interest lighting her eyes. "Christina!" Molly exclaimed, as if some idea had just popped into her head.

"Hi, Molly," Christina answered politely.

Molly nodded and smiled, her small mouth making a tight little U-shape on her heart-shaped face. Christina had never seen a smile convey so little warmth. "You *work* here, Christina?" Molly asked.

"Yep," Christina said, wondering where all this was going.

Molly's smile grew even tighter as she leaned forward. "Could you do something about this awful old nag they stuck me with?"

Inwardly, Christina cringed. She hoped old Elmer, the sweet-tempered horse Molly was on, couldn't understand what she'd said. Christina figured he probably couldn't, but sometimes she wondered. Some of the horses seemed so human, and Elmer was one of them. To Christina, his black eyes seemed to shine with intelligence.

She patted Elmer's side. "He's a good horse. You'll like him once you get going," she told Molly reassuringly. She was really addressing her encouraging words to Elmer.

A look of fiery anger flashed in Molly's dark eyes.

Christina turned away before she could say anything else and hurried into the stable, where Ashley was already saddling May, a palomino mare.

Her mother was brushing down a deep brown mare

named Bridey. "Here are you gloves, Mom," Christina said, handing over the leather gloves. "Can I take Bridey out for a ride?"

"I suppose she's ready to go," her mother said, patting the horse affectionately on her side.

"Hi, girl," Christina spoke to the horse.

"What did Miss Pine Ridge Country Club want?" Ashley asked acidly as she adjusted the stirrup length on a saddle she'd slung over a stable door.

"She doesn't want to ride Elmer," Christina told her.

"Oh, sure," Ashley fumed. "She knows you when she wants a favor. That's just like her."

Katie stood with her arms folded, a serious expression on her face, studying the different horses. "Which one should I ride?" she asked.

"Try Daisy," Alice told Katie, pointing to a gray horse. "She's a nice old girl. You won't have any trouble with her. She knows the trail, and she's very calm. Hold on a minute, and I'll saddle her for you."

Christina saddled Bridey while her mother readied Daisy for Katie.

"Here," Alice said, handing Katie Daisy's reins. "Lead her out."

Daisy sputtered and neighed softly.

"Whoa! Nice horsie," Katie spoke edgily as she walked toward the door with Daisy, who clopped calmly behind her.

Christina led Bridey from her stall while Ashley took May from the stall next door.

"You don't have to be nervous riding Daisy. She's great," Ashley reassured Katie, who waited at the stable door holding Daisy's reins. "Daisy isn't a thing like Bridey," Ashley continued. "Bridey's so temperamental. I don't know why you always want to ride her, Christina."

"She and I understand each other," Christina said with a laugh. "She's cool for me most of the time."

"That's true, she is," Ashley agreed.

They led the horses outside and mounted them. "All set!" Ashley told her father.

"All right, let's head out," Mr. Kingsley called to the group.

"Wait!" Molly shouted sharply. "Nobody move!"

4

"What's wrong?" asked Mr. Kingsley mildly, turning in his saddle to face Molly.

"I refuse to ride this horse. No offense, but he looks like he's about to drop dead," Molly said in an arrogant, demanding tone of voice.

Mrs. Morgan, on the horse beside Molly, looked embarrassed but said nothing.

"He's a very good horse," Mr. Kingsley said firmly.

"This isn't the first time I've ridden, you know," Molly insisted indignantly. "I don't want an old, broken-down horse."

"She *is* an excellent rider," Mrs. Morgan murmured.

"How about that horse?" Molly suggested, pointing to Bridey. "I like the look of that one. At least it looks like a horse with some spirit."

"In case you didn't notice, that horse already has

someone on it," Katie muttered sarcastically.

Molly glanced briefly in Katie's direction and turned back, as if Katie were a droning mosquito who had fleetingly distracted her.

"It's all right," Christina said, swinging one long leg over Bridey's saddle as she dismounted. "But, Molly, Bridey can be difficult sometimes."

"I can handle horses, believe me," Molly said confidently, getting off Elmer. "I've ridden dressage for *years*."

"All right," Christina agreed. "I just thought I ought to warn you, is all."

"Wait a minute there, now girls," Mr. Kingsley cut in. "*I* don't think she should ride Bridey."

A condescending laugh burst out of Mrs. Morgan. "Oh, please, Mr. Kingsley, my daughter is an excellent horsewoman. She's used to horses. We're only here because the stables at the club close in August. Everyone leaves town and takes their horses with them. I'm afraid I really must insist she have the horse of her choosing."

Mr. Kingsley looked as if he was about to say something, and then seemed to change his mind. "All right," he agreed reluctantly.

Molly climbed onto Bridey while Christina got on Elmer. The group headed toward the Pine Manor Woods, which bordered the ranch.

The moment they entered the woods, Christina inhaled the deep pine scent. The tall evergreens swayed gently overhead, nearly blocking out the sky except for shifting shards of bright light that filtered down through the branches. The dry warmth of the air out by the ranch gave way to the dense, moist coolness of the forest.

A light breeze tickled the back of Christina's neck. She shivered a little and clicked softly to Elmer, encouraging him to keep up with the others on the trail. Molly had been right about one thing. Elmer *was* slow, but he was a nice, gentle horse.

They rode on through the woods at an easy pace. Elmer fell to the very last place in the line, behind May and Bridey, who trotted together, side by side.

"Are you all right back there?" Ashley called over her shoulder.

"Fine," Christina replied, smiling.

As the line continued, Christina and Elmer fell farther and farther behind. Ashley checked from time to time, but Christina was an experienced rider, and Elmer was a very tame horse. There was no reason to worry.

Lulled by the steady clip-clop of hoofbeats, Christina soon began to daydream about her upcoming ballet lessons. From what she'd heard at school, they weren't too expensive. Even if she had to pitch in some money from her allowance, she was pretty sure her mother could afford to send her.

Christina imagined herself dancing in the woods, leaping and kicking, barefoot and graceful among the trees. In her daydream, she wore a gossamer gown of spring green, and flowers adorned her flowing hair. A heavenly singing from some unknown source filled the air. Christina imagined herself leaping so high her hair brushed the piney fingers of the uppermost branches, as if she were actually flying with invisible, angelic wings.

Before too long, Christina heard the burbling rush of water that told her they were near the creek. The wide path of water cut through the woods, rambling this way and that.

It was the same creek spanned at one point by the Angels Crossing Bridge. This old-fashioned covered bridge was where, several months earlier, Katie had first encountered three angels and then brought them to help Ashley and Christina.

Ever since then, Christina had felt different in a way she couldn't explain, not even to Ashley or Katie. Not even to herself.

She knew not everyone got to see angels. But, now that she'd had the experience, she knew beyond doubt that angels were real. A force for good and love *was* alive in the world. Christina had always suspected that good, mystical forces were at work in the universe. Now she knew for sure.

She felt now, as never before, that she could take risks and try for things that might once have seemed impossible. Things like becoming a ballerina.

As a small child, she'd dreamed of dancing in a grand ballet company even though ballet lessons never seemed to be possible.

Christina and her mother had moved around a lot when she was little. Christina's father had left them when she was a baby. She didn't remember him at all. Before coming to the ranch, her mother had had difficulty finding work she liked. So they'd gone from place to place. They'd never settled anywhere for long.

Then, when Christina was about five, they'd come to the ranch. And stayed. Her mother had said maybe Christina could have ballet lessons once she'd paid off some money she owed, and then after she'd saved enough to buy a car. By the time all that happened, Christina was caught up in the world of horses there at the ranch. She was busy learning to ride, to groom, and to tend horses.

She forgot about ballet, for the most part. When she *did* think about it, she got scared. Other girls she knew who took ballet had been studying it for years. How could she ever catch up with them? It was too late. She'd missed her chance.

Now, though, she didn't care. The angels would help her, guide her. Seeing *Swan Lake* had reawakened all her old dreams.

Now Christina was awakened from her thoughts by the sound of voices shouting. She looked up sharply to see what was happening.

Bridey had broken loose from the group. She galloped wildly up a hill with Molly desperately clutching her neck. "Help!" she screamed as she began slipping from the saddle.

Christina tightened the reins and leaned forward in the saddle. "Come on," she told Elmer, squeezing his side with her knees. Elmer broke into a run as Christina headed him up the hill after Molly.

5

"Molly!" Christina shouted from the top of the hill.

At the bottom, beside the creek, Molly struggled with Bridey. The horse turned in furious, frustrated circles as the girl pulled hard on her reins, her long braid whipping in the air.

"Loosen the reins!" Christina shouted, heading down the hill.

Molly didn't seem to hear her. She yanked up harder on the reins, causing Bridey to back into the rushing water of the creek. The water swirled at Bridey's feet, spooking the unhappy mare even more.

"Whoa, Bridey!" Christina shouted as she neared the water. "Easy, girl."

"Do something!" Molly screamed, her face flushed and her eyes wide with fright.

Bridey hadn't responded to Christina's voice. She was

afraid the horse might slip as it bucked angrily in the water.

With a shrill whinny, Bridey reared back.

Molly lost hold of the reins and grabbed frantically at the horse's black mane.

"Come on, Elmer," Christina said as she headed Elmer into the cold, rushing water. "Easy girl, easy," she cooed as she neared the frantic Bridey. She stretched forward to grab Bridey's flying reins. Just as her fingertips touched the flying leather, Bridey abruptly reared back.

Christina couldn't grab the reins in time. "Oh, no!" Christina gasped as Molly pitched backward into the air.

Everything happened quickly after that.

Molly hit the water with an enormous splash.

Mr. Kingsley and Ashley rushed into the creek.

Christina had been so involved in what she was doing that she hadn't even noticed them coming over the hill after her. Now she recovered Bridey as the entire group of riders sat on their horses at the edge of the water watching. Some dismounted, anxious to help. Mrs. Morgan was already off her horse, running back and forth along the water's edge.

Molly sputtered and gasped as she struggled to her feet. The water pushed her back as it rushed past her. Mr. Kingsley fished the girl out of the water, pulling her up from under her armpits.

"Are you all right, Molly?" Ashley asked. She had waded into the water alongside her father.

Molly's shoulders heaved while she worked to regain her breath. Strands of her long hair lay plastered to her face, which shone bright red.

"What happened?" Mr. Kingsley asked.

"That stupid horse is crazy," Molly spit out the words angrily. "I was trying to her get under control."

"I thought you were experienced," Ashley said.

Molly looked up sharply at Christina. "It's her fault!" she accused. "I had the horse under control until she came along and started yanking the reins."

Christina's jaw dropped. She was too stunned to speak.

Molly sloshed furiously through the water until she reached her mother on the water's edge. "Why didn't you tell us that horse was so wild?" Mrs. Morgan shrilled. She took off her lightweight cardigan sweater and wrapped it around Molly's wet shoulders. "I can't believe the lack of responsibility on your part."

"You said she was an experienced rider," Mr. Kingsley said angrily. "When I tried to keep her from riding Bridey, you insisted she be allowed to do so!"

"I *am* an experienced rider!" Molly said indignantly. "That horse is insane!"

"Oh, get off it," Katie said. She had dismounted. "Bridey isn't insane and you know it!"

"I know what happened," Molly muttered darkly, glaring at Christina. "*She* certainly didn't help matters."

"I was trying to calm Bridey," Christina said, finding her voice at last.

Molly looked at the other riders, and streaks of pink mottled her face. Christina could tell she was mortified. Everyone had seen her fall into the creek.

"Let's just make sure you're okay," Mr. Kingsley said evenly. He had Molly move her head slowly, then her arms and legs. She grumbled but didn't seem to be seriously hurt.

"Come on, everyone," Mr. Kingsley said calmly. "Ashley, you lead the trail. Christina, you can take up the rear. I'm heading back for the ranch with Mrs. Morgan and her daughter."

"I'm not getting back on that animal!" Molly exclaimed warningly.

Now calmed, Bridey had come alongside Elmer. "I'll ride Bridey, and you take Elmer back," Christina suggested.

"Good idea," Mr. Kingsley said.

"You can't let a young girl ride that beast," Mrs. Morgan argued. "How can you, after what just happened?"

Christina guided Bridey alongside her and she and Elmer left the creek. She dismounted from Elmer and climbed onto Bridey.

"Christina can handle Bridey," Ashley informed Mrs. Morgan. "That's why she was on her in the first place."

Dripping and red-faced, Molly climbed onto Elmer. She glowered at Christina, her eyes filled with fury.

"Christina will be fine. She's very experienced," Mr. Kingsley told Mrs. Morgan.

"I'm experienced, too," Molly insisted sourly.

"Yes, but not, as we know, on Bridey. Let's get back to the ranch," Mr. Kingsley said briskly.

With Ashley in the lead, the main group headed back up the hill as Mr. Kingsley went off with Molly and her mother. "I expect a full refund," Mrs. Morgan's voice sounded even after she was no longer in sight.

"That was so funny!" Katie laughed, trotting along beside Christina. "What a goof on Molly, Miss Experienced Rider." She lifted her chin and assumed an arrogant expression as she imitated Molly. "I've ridden dressage." Katie tossed back her hair and laughed. "Oh, give me a break. 'Dressage.'"

"I wonder what got Bridey so crazy," Christina mused.

"You've always said she's a difficult horse," Katie reminded her.

"Yes, but still . . . I've never seen her act like *that.* I wonder if she was reacting to Molly's aura."

"Her *what*?" Katie yelped.

"*Aura.* You know, the circle of light and energy that surrounds each one of us."

Katie shook her head mournfully. "No, no. Please don't start with that crazy stuff again. I can't take it."

"It's not crazy," Christina told her firmly. "Molly is not a nice person, and that shows up in a person's aura. The aura of mean people can be small or have a strange color. I think animals are very sensitive to auras."

"Get out of here," Katie scoffed.

Christina wasn't surprised by Katie's reaction. Katie thought anything mystical or unexplainable was just nonsense. She didn't believe in horoscopes, tarot cards, or crystal power. Of the three friends, she was the one who'd had the hardest time believing they'd really seen angels. Afterward, she'd even tried to insist they'd imagined them, even though she'd been the first one to see them in the woods and later they'd really helped her when she needed it.

Now Katie admitted the angels were real, but she refused to acknowledge that there was anything special or mysterious about the woods. Christina knew differently. She could feel that it was an ancient, magical place, full of amazing power spots.

Power spots were places rich with positive energy from the earth. They were good places where life flourished. Some people said power spots were gateways to the spirit world.

Christina believed the old Angels Crossing Bridge was built over a huge power spot. That was why they could sometimes find the angels there.

Katie didn't believe there was any such thing as a power spot. It wasn't all that surprising that she didn't want to hear about auras, either.

"Yes," Christina said aloud, more to herself than to Katie. "It must have been Molly's aura. Bridey sensed a bad aura and wanted it off her back."

"It wasn't that," Katie insisted. "I saw what happened. Bridey started wandering off the path a little, like she wanted to go somewhere. Molly tried to stop her by yanking the reins."

"Where was she going?" Christina asked curiously.

"Toward a patch of sunlight, I think," Katie said.

Christina looked at her sharply. "A power spot!" she gasped.

"Oh, stop it!" Katie said irritably. "It was just sun."

"I've never seen Bridey care about a patch of sunlight," Christina insisted. "It had to have been something else."

They continued along the trail as it rose ever higher, climbing to a narrow, rocky ridge where, above the treetops, they could view the rolling fields and lush pine forests that were home to the rural community of Pine Ridge.

Ashley stopped the group to give everyone a moment to take in the spectacular view. "Wow, it's really beautiful up here," Katie sighed.

"It is," Christina agreed, nodding. "I've always loved to come up here." Whenever she looked out over this expanse and drank in its sheer beauty, Christina was again reminded that there was more to life than the everyday things her five senses revealed. At those times, she knew—beyond even the smallest doubt—that there were dimensions to life that weren't as available to the senses, but that were just as real. She felt it deep in her heart.

"You know," Katie said quietly, "maybe it has to do with physics."

"What are you talking about?" Christina asked.

"All the weird things you believe in," Katie replied, gazing out at the landscape. "Spirits, crystals, auras, and all that junk."

"What do you mean?"

"Well, I'm not sure how to explain it," Katie began. "I was watching this weird new cable channel the other day. The Science Channel, I think it was called. Anyway, they had this program on, all about Einstein and his theories. You know, how matter vibrates at different energy levels and how if you went fast enough, you might even be able to travel backward in time."

"I don't understand," Christina admitted.

"Neither did I," Katie said. "But it got me thinking. I mean, maybe the world works in ways we can't understand yet. What if a ghost is really just someone who has started to vibrate so fast that you can barely see him or her—kind of like the way you can barely see a hummingbird's wings because they beat so quickly?"

Christina looked hard at Katie. "Are you thinking about your parents?" she asked.

Katie nodded. "Sometimes I have this feeling that they're around me. I know it's crazy, but . . . That show got me thinking, that's all."

"Anything is possible," Christina said with a nod. Now, more than ever before, she felt anything at all was possible.

On the return trip to the stable, Ashley led the group back the same way they'd come.

When they were almost halfway there, Katie came close to Christina. "Be careful," she warned, "just up ahead is where Bridey bolted."

"Thanks," Christina replied.

Slowing down, Christina scanned the woods, looking for a patch of strange sunshine or anything else that might have spooked Bridey. She didn't see anything that seemed peculiar.

Ashley, Katie, and the rest of the group were a little ahead of her now, about five yards. Suddenly Bridey whinnied and began pulling to the left.

"Whoa, girl, where are you going?" Christina asked the horse.

Bridey continued going to the left. Christina would have let her go, just to see where she'd head, but she was supposed to be riding backup for the group. She adjusted the reins, gently trying to steer Bridey back onto the path. Bridey fought her.

"Come on, Bridey," Christina coaxed. "Come on."

A warm breeze blew Christina's hair back. *What was happening?* she wondered.

Bridey neighed and stomped her forelegs.

Christina tightened the reins, pulling Bridey's bit. Still the horse resisted her.

Before she knew it, they were turning in a circle.

Then, suddenly, Bridey stopped and whinnied. Christina gasped. A spot of brilliant sunlight had opened up in the woods a few yards ahead of where they stood.

Christina stared at it hard.

Shimmering in the light was the outline of a human figure. A human figure with wings!

6

Entranced by the vision before her, Christina loosened her grip on the reins. Bridey walked slowly forward.

The luminous being grew brighter. Christina couldn't make out the details of the figure. She tried to urge Bridey forward faster. She had to get closer.

When Christina thought she'd gotten close enough, she discovered the glowing patch still hung just out of reach—although it hadn't seemed to move at all.

The balmy breeze continued to surround Christina, gently rustling her hair and warming her face.

Without any commands from Christina, Bridey followed the shimmering figure as it floated placidly through the woods. Christina forgot all about following up the end of the line. She forgot about everything. Instead she surrendered herself to the feeling of enchantment and let Bridey carry her along.

With her eyes locked on the apparition before her, Christina was dimly aware that Bridey was carrying her up a hill. She heard the sound of running water and knew that, once again, they were near the creek. At the top of the hill, Bridey stopped a moment.

Christina looked down at the old covered bridge spanning the creek at the bottom of the hill. Whatever road had once led to the bridge had long since been engulfed by the pine forest. "Angels Crossing," Christina murmured.

The shining circle of light hovered at the entrance of the bridge.

Bridey descended the hill.

Just as they reached the entrance of the bridge, the figure seemed to dip under the roof of the bridge.

Bridey's footsteps echoed as she clopped along the bridge's worn wooden floor. Christina realized the angel—for she had no doubt that it was an angel—was leading them somewhere.

But where?

Christina had never traveled this deeply into the woods before. She lost all sense of time as they continued on. She didn't know if they'd been traveling for minutes or hours. The woods seemed to change as they went deeper and deeper into it. The pines were thicker and closer together. Little sunshine filtered down through the canopy of branches above. Everything was cast in a misty twilight, neither day nor night but something in between.

The mat of pine needles and moss beneath them was so thick that Bridey's footsteps were completely silent. The air was rich with the heady scent of pine.

The angel led them over another hill. As they crested the hill, Bridey stopped once again. Below them was a small, rough wooden house. Its roof sagged. Some of the windows had cardboard taped over them.

In the yard, a thick black tire swing hung from the branch of a spindly pine. Piles of wood had been chopped and stacked neatly to one side. An old-fashioned, rust colored pump stood near the entrance to the house.

The angel hovered in the yard, and Christina had the feeling that they'd arrived at their destination. Bridey carried Christina closer to the house.

Suddenly a young man of about seventeen or eighteen came out of the house.

In a blink the angel disappeared.

Shocked, Christina gasped and accidentally pulled back on Bridey's reins. Bridey whinnied in annoyance.

The young man looked at them sharply. "Hey!" he shouted aggressively. "What are you doing here?"

That was when Christina saw the slingshot he carried at his side.

"Nothing. Nothing," she sputtered, seized with panic.

With a slap to Bridey's side, she turned the horse around and raced back up the hill at a gallop. She didn't stop running until she sighted the creek and the Angels Crossing Bridge.

As she crossed the bridge, Christina heard voices in

the distance—voices calling her name.

On the other side of the bridge she saw Ashley and Katie on horseback coming toward her. "There she is!" Ashley cried.

"What happened to you?" Katie asked when they came alongside Christina. "I thought you were right behind and then suddenly I turned around, and you were gone."

"I . . . I . . . I saw an angel, and I followed it," Christina told them.

"What?" Ashley gasped.

Christina told them exactly what had happened.

"It's a good thing you got out of there!" Ashley exclaimed.

"Why would an angel bother to lead you to some guy with a slingshot?" Katie wondered aloud.

"I don't know," Christina said. "I have no idea."

7

Christina couldn't stop thinking about the angel in the woods. Why had it led her to that house and that guy? What did it mean? What was going on? Could she even be sure it *was* an angel?

The question niggled at her for days, but slowly she began to let it go. Her attention shifted to Amy's Academy of Dance. "Please, Mom, the summer session starts this week. You have to decide," she pleaded late one afternoon as they walked home from the stable together.

"Yes. All right," Alice agreed. "I guess we can afford it. Since you want it so badly," she added.

Christina threw her arms around her mother. Then she raced ahead to the cabin. She wanted to call Amy's Academy right away.

Amy warned her that it was late in the summer session to begin class. "You'll have to be ready for our recital. That's at the end of August. Less than four weeks away," she stressed.

"I'll learn the steps," Christina assured her.

Christina could barely sit still for the few days until class started. Her eagerness and excitement were almost more than she could stand.

"Oh, Ashley, wish me luck," she said the evening before class began as they sat together on the fence along the horse pasture. "I hope I can do this. I want to so badly."

"Then you'll do it," Ashley said confidently.

Christina folded her arms and drew in a long shaky breath. What would tomorrow be like? It was as if her future was about to begin. She'd found her calling. And it was all thanks to the angels. She was embarking on a path she would have been too afraid to try—if she hadn't been inspired.

From now on everything would be different for Christina. She knew it would. Her life would revolve around ballet.

That night, Christina couldn't sleep. She paced her room anxiously. Over and over she checked her shopping bag to make sure she had everything she needed: leotard, tights, ballet slippers.

Holding the bag to her heart she sat in the tall-back rocker by her window and stared out at the clear, starry night sky. The rocking motion calmed her and soon her head fell forward as she drifted to sleep.

A dream came to her. In her dream she was dressed

in a soft petal pink dress, her blonde hair loose. She danced slowly, each of her movements a perfectly executed ballet step. Beautiful, strange music filled the woods. As she turned in a graceful circle she spied a young man several yards away. He wore jeans and a loose white shirt. He danced a fast step and then bounded into the air, higher than she'd ever seen any ballet dancer leap. Her heart thrilled to his dance.

Christina stopped her own dance to watch him, fascinated. Then, lightly as she'd been dancing a moment earlier, she leaped toward him. She reached out and felt his fingers brush hers as he spun just out of reach—and disappeared.

Christina blinked. There he was again, a few yards ahead this time, still dancing. Christina tried reaching out a second time. Again he disappeared.

When he appeared again in a different spot, he was laughing. Not taunting, but a good-natured, warm laugh. He beckoned to her to come closer. Christina stepped forward, then stopped to listen. She could hear a ringing in the distance. It was growing louder.

Christina sat up in her rocker suddenly. It was her alarm clock. "Oh, my gosh!" she cried. "This is it!"

This morning she started at Amy's Academy!

Christina drove with her mother in their pickup truck. "I'll see you in an hour," Alice said as Christina climbed out in front of the post office. To the right of the post office was a door with a heart-shaped sign hanging above it that read: Amy's Academy of Dance.

Waving to her mother, Christina opened the door and began climbing the narrow wooden stairs leading to the dance studio.

When Christina reached the top landing, she saw girls hurrying back and forth. Some brushed their hair, some smoothed their leotards. All looked perfect and poised.

She noticed two girls dressed in matching black leotards and pink tights seated on a brocade-covered loveseat. They were intently tying up the bows on their soft, black leather ballet slippers.

Christina's eyes were fixed on the slippers. She clutched her bag more tightly and softly bit her lip. Her own slippers were pink. She'd called the school to find out what she needed, but she didn't remember being told to get black slippers.

The pink slippers would have to do, Christina told herself. This was too meaningful an endeavor to let the wrong color shoes throw her off her stride. She'd have to rise above that kind of silly self-consciousness. Something much more important was at stake.

Christina followed two girls holding dance bags into the changing room, an open space with rows of pink lockers and a long white wooden bench down the middle. It smelled of perfume, baby powder, and new paint.

She looked around for anyone she might know from school but didn't see a familiar face. Instead, she felt invisible. None of the other girls even smiled or said hello. They were all involved in pulling on tights or arranging their hair. They chatted together in small clusters. No one paid the slightest attention to Christina.

Most of the girls had long hair tied in ponytails or coiled into casually elegant chignons. Christina's own long, blonde hair was loose, and she had nothing with which to tie it back.

Selecting an empty locker, Christina pulled it open and began to change. In the next three minutes, as she pulled on her pink tights, girls left the room one by one as if signaled by some silent bell. Christina was reminded of a flock of starlings that had once landed together beside the stable and then, all at the same time, taken off and flown into the woods.

Christina sat on the bench and pulled on her pink shoes. Dim late-afternoon sunlight came in from the one window in the corner. She gazed at the wavery light and wondered if an angel was with her now, watching her, helping her. Or did they only come if there was a crisis?

She got up from the bench, taking a long, nervous breath. "Well, wish me luck," she said to a patch of light, just in case an angel was actually standing in that spot.

Outside, on the bright, sunny dance floor, eighteen young dancers sat cross-legged on the shiny floor while the teacher, a slim, blonde young woman, took attendance. "Christina Kramer," she called.

"Here!" Christina hurried out to join the others.

"Hello," the instructor greeted Christina. "I'm Amy. Have you danced before, Christina?"

"No. I mean, I've never had lessons. I learned a Native American dance last summer, when my mother and I visited a reservation, but that's not what you mean, is it?"

"No," Amy said pleasantly. "I meant ballet."

"This is my first ballet class," Christina admitted.

"You'll have some catching up to do, then," Amy told her. "Just watch the others. I'll help you when I can. You'll catch on."

"Okay."

"And you'll need black slippers for the recital in August, so you might want to get them now," Amy added. The entire class glanced at Christina's feet. She felt as if the pink slippers were glowing.

After attendance, the girls went to the barre, which ran along three sides of the room. The room's fourth side was covered entirely by a huge mirror. "Let's start our warm-up with demi-pliés in first position," Amy said to the class.

Christina has no idea what Amy was talking about, but she watched the other girls place one hand gracefully on the barre and position their feet with the heels touching and tried to imitate them.

Amy turned on the stereo. Soothing classical music filled the room. "Let's begin," said Amy. "One and . . ."

"Sorry I'm late," a girl said, rushing into the room.

Christina looked up. It was Molly Morgan. *Just great!* Christina thought bitterly. *The one person here I know turns out to be Molly!*

As she took her place at the barre, Molly shot a glance at Christina. It was hard to tell if it registered surprise or annoyance. Maybe a mixture of both.

Amy led the class in their warm-up for several minutes. As she did, she walked around the class, correcting the girls' positions—straightening shoulders, lifting a chin, encouraging some girls to turn their feet out farther. When she got to Christina, she stayed for nearly five full minutes. "You're slumping," she told Christina. "Pretend you have an invisible string in the middle of your head and it's lifting you to the ceiling."

Self-consciously, Christina tried straightening up.

"Don't hunch your shoulders," Amy said. "And keep those feet turned out."

Christina did her best to keep Amy's words in mind, but just looking in the mirror she could see she had it all wrong. Her rear end seemed to stick out impossibly far, while the other girls stood perfectly straight. She tried to remember to keep her shoulders back, but the moment she began concentrating on positioning her feet, she forgot about her shoulders.

Every time she checked herself in the mirror, she wanted to disappear. She felt gawky and awkward, while the others were all incredibly graceful. Adding to her self-consciousness and embarrassment was the fact that she always seemed to be up when they were down. Somehow she always managed to be one, two, or even three steps behind the group. It was awful.

Once, she happened to glance at Molly in the mirror,

and their eyes met in the reflection. Molly's face was fixed in a smirky, mocking smile. Christina turned away, mortified.

After a few minutes of vainly trying to keep up, Christina's concentration began to wander. That was when she realized something truly awful.

She was the heaviest girl in the whole class—the tallest and definitely the heaviest!

Realizing this surprised Christina so much that she stumbled into the girl in front of her. "Ow!" cried the girl as she fell into the girl in front of her.

The entire class stopped practicing and turned to see what had happened. "What's wrong?" Amy asked, rushing over to them.

"She fell on me," the girl Christina had knocked into complained petulantly.

"Sorry," Christina said, filled with embarrassment.

"All right. Get back in step," Amy instructed the class. "Arabesques from second position."

Christina struggled through the rest of the warm-up. *You're new. You'll catch up*, she told herself. But what could she do about her body? That wouldn't be as easy to change. It might even be impossible to change.

It was a new idea to Christina that there might be anything wrong with her body. She'd always thought of herself as slim—willowy, even. Many people even considered her skinny. But there was no denying it. Ranged alongside her in the merciless mirror, every single other girl in the class had a slenderer profile than

Christina. She began to feel ungainly. Big and horsey. It was a terrible feeling.

You're just being self-conscious and ridiculous, she scolded herself sternly. She knew people born in her astrological sign, Aquarius, always wanted everything to be perfect. They could be especially hard on themselves. *That's what you're doing now*, she told herself. *Just forget about it, and stop being so self-centered.*

Amy turned off the stereo. "All right, girls," she told the class. "Find your spots for floor work."

The girls left the barre and spaced themselves around the room. They all seemed to have a spot, a regular place. Christina gazed around, trying to find a place to fit herself into the group.

As she searched, someone brushed against her elbow. She turned and found herself face to face with Molly. "Clumsy moose," Molly whispered nastily before walking on to her place in the center of the dance studio.

8

Christina stood in front of the full-length mirror on the back of her bedroom door. Dressed only in her plain white underwear, she studied her shape.

Broad shoulders. Long, strong legs.

She turned sideways. Her tummy could be flatter. Christina sucked in her stomach. "That's better."

But she couldn't hold her breath forever.

Christina jumped at a sudden loud knock at her bedroom door.

"It's me, Ashley," came the voice from the other side of the door.

Grabbing her robe from the bed and throwing it on, Christina let Ashley in. "Hi," Ashley said, coming into the room and bouncing onto Christina's bed. "I knocked on the front door, but no one answered. So I just came in. I saw you come home a while ago."

"That's okay."

"How was your first ballet class?"

"Terrible," Christina said bluntly as she plopped onto the bed beside Ashley. "I couldn't keep up. I had *no* idea what was going on. And Molly Morgan is in the class. It's hard to pay attention with her there. She's just waiting for me to make a mistake so she can smirk at me. Like she did today."

"Bummer," Ashley sympathized.

"Besides that, I look like a giant blob compared with the other girls."

"You are *not* a blob!" Ashley said emphatically.

"The girls in class are all thin and graceful. I feel like a total clod."

"Don't say that about yourself," Ashley insisted. "You're beautiful, Christina. You have a great shape."

Christina glanced at herself in the mirror. Before today, she'd liked her looks. All her life people had told her she was pretty.

She even liked the small white scar that cut through her left eyebrow. The scar dated from years ago, when she was first learning to ride. She'd been thrown from a pony. Of course it had hurt at the time, but now she thought the scar gave her pale face character.

Despite the confidence she'd once felt about her looks, Christina wasn't quite at home in her body yet. She'd grown and changed so rapidly in the last two years.

As a child she'd been reed-thin. But that was changing, and she wasn't sure she liked the direction these changes were taking. "I wish I was petite, like you," she told Ashley.

"Trust me, you don't want to be a shrimp like me," Ashley disagreed with assurance.

"You're not a shrimp. No way! You're just petite and cute," Christina laughed. "You'd fit right into that dance class. But I'm like a . . . a . . . moose."

"Give me a break," Ashley scoffed. "You look like the girl in the Guess jeans ad."

"I do not," Christina grumbled sullenly.

"Why don't you forget about your thighs and come to the mall with me," Ashley suggested.

"It's my stomach and rear that are the problem, not my thighs," Christina replied. "But now that you mention it, my thighs are sort of on the thick side."

Ashley snapped up a sweatshirt draped over Christina's bedpost and tossed it playfully at Christina. "Come on. Get dressed and stop worrying about nothing."

Dressing quickly, Christina realized talking to Ashley had made her feel better. "Ready," she said as she ran a brush through her hair. "How are we getting there?"

"Jeremy," Ashley said, referring to one of her twin older brothers. "He's going there to meet some friends, and he said he'd give us a ride."

It took almost a half hour to get to the Pine Ridge Mall outside of town. Christina and Ashley said good-bye to tall, red-haired Jeremy and went off to browse in the stores.

At Jensen's Department Store they were looking

through the new spring clothing when Christina froze, her heart pounding.

A tall, good-looking boy with long brown hair and wire-rim glasses stood looking at sports sweatshirts with two other boys from their class at school, Darrin Tyson and Mike Jones. It was Matt Larson, the boy Christina had a crush on.

"Look. It's Matt," Christina told Ashley.

Ashley looked up and gasped sharply. "Your horoscope. It was right! This is your chance to talk to him. It's perfect. I can't *be-lievvve* it!"

"I can't do it," Christina said, suddenly overwhelmed with shyness.

Christina hadn't known Matt since grammar school, as she had most of the other kids in her class. He'd come to Pine Ridge Middle School the previous year, in the seventh grade. So even though she knew Matt—sort of—Christina didn't feel as at ease with him as she felt with most of her classmates.

Still, ever since last September, Christina hadn't been able to help noticing how cute Matt was. He seemed nice, too. All year she'd hoped to get to know him better.

Ashley grabbed Christina's wrist. "Come on," she said, dragging her forward toward the boys. "This is the chance you've been waiting for."

Christina's palms began to get clammy and wet as she let herself be pulled along. "What will we say to them? We need a reason to go over there."

"No, we don't," Ashley disagreed.

"Yes, we do," Christina insisted anxiously.

"I'll think of something."

Christina smiled nervously as they neared the boys.

"Hey, Darrin!" Ashley said to the boy with the short, blond hair. "Hi, guys."

The boys looked over at them and nodded in greeting.

"What's happening?" Darrin asked.

"Duh, we're shopping," Ashley said. "Listen, I came over to ask you something. I need to get a present for my dad. He really likes basketball, and I was thinking of getting him a team sweatshirt or something. What's a good team, do you think?"

"Chicago Bulls," Darrin said instantly.

"No way," Mike countered. "It's the Knicks, the New York Knicks."

"The Bulls rule," Darrin insisted.

"What do you think?" Ashley asked Matt daringly. "Want to be the tiebreaker?"

"Uh," Matt cleared his throat. "I'm, uh, not a big basketball fan. I'm, uh, more into soccer."

The conversation fizzled out for an uncomfortable few seconds. They stood looking at one another. Matt gave Christina a quick, edgy smile. She smiled back then gazed down self-consciously at the tile floor.

"So," said Ashley, firing up the conversation again. "What are you guys doing?"

"Just hanging around," Mike told them.

Say something, Christina urged herself. *Don't stand here like a dope.* But she couldn't think of anything to say.

"Hey, Christina, I liked your column in the school paper," Matt spoke unexpectedly.

Christina's skin tingled with excitement. This was great! He liked the horoscope column she wrote for the paper! "You did?" she said happily. "Th-hanks."

"It was a great column, wasn't it?" Ashley said enthusiastically. "Now that it's summer, I have to go back to reading the one in the newspaper, and it's not nearly as good. I'm lucky, though," she babbled on. "Christina did my entire astrological chart last year. She's a wiz at astrology. What sign are you, Matt?"

"Libra, I think."

"Me, too!" Ashley cried. "What a coincidence. That means you'd get along very well with Christina. She and I became friends the first moment we met. Isn't that right, Christina?"

"Yes," Christina agreed honestly.

Christina hoped Matt hadn't picked up on Ashley's obvious attempt to match them up. She didn't want him to think she had put Ashley up to it.

In a way she was embarrassed that Ashley was being so pushy, but she was grateful, too. She was breaking the ice in a way Christina would never have been able to do on her own.

"We were just about to eat some lunch at Burger Broil upstairs," Ashley said. "Want to come?"

"Okay," Matt answered first.

"I guess so," Mike agreed.

The group rode the escalator to the second floor of

the mall. At Burger Broil, everyone ordered burgers except Christina. She'd decided a while back that she just couldn't stand to eat anything that had a face. It just didn't seem right to her. She ordered a salad.

"Are you a vegetarian?" Matt asked Christina as they brought their food to a table.

"No way," said Darrin. "I bet you're on a diet, right, Christina?"

"I'm *not* on a diet," Christina replied indignantly. *That stupid Darrin!* Christina thought angrily. Why did he have to say that in front of Matt? "I *am* a vegetarian."

"Since when?" Darrin asked skeptically. "You and Ashley were flipping burgers on the grill at the firehouse picnic last August."

"You should know," Ashley said smartly. "You ate most of them."

"Did not," Darrin disagreed. "I saw you and the vegetarian here chowing down every chance you got."

"I just recently became a vegetarian," Christina told him huffily as she sat at the table and opened her cardboard container of salad.

"You don't look like a salad eater," Matt said, biting into his burger.

A piece of lettuce caught in Christina's throat, making her cough.

She didn't look like a salad eater!

What does he mean by that? she wondered as she coughed. What did he think salad eaters looked like, anyway?

Suddenly, with a sick feeling of certainty, Christina knew what Matt was really trying to say.

He thought she was fat!

9

"Christina, cut it out! Would you please stop saying you're fat!" Katie cried in exasperation. "I'm sick of hearing it!"

"Well, I'm sick of *being* it," Christina replied.

"Christina, you are *not* fat!" Ashley cried. Her pretty face, too, was creased with exasperation.

"What does it take to get through to you?" Katie marveled as Christina stubbornly ignored them.

"Look, are you coming in with me, or not?" Christina asked calmly.

They stood at the front of the Pine Ridge Pharmacy. Katie and Ashley had reluctantly agreed to take the bus into town with Christina.

She wanted to buy diet aids.

It had been nearly a week since what Christina thought of as the disastrous encounter with Matt at the mall. She couldn't stop replaying the whole conversation again and again in her head. And every time, she could only come up with one explanation of why he'd said what he did. He thought she was fat.

Christina had also had a second ballet class since then. It had gone just as badly as the first—maybe even worse, because this time Christina hadn't been able to concentrate at all. Her entire attention had been absorbed by the slim, graceful images of the other girls reflected in the mirror—and on how horsey and lumpy she, Christina, looked in comparison. Nothing she did could ever look nearly as elegant—at least, not until she slimmed down.

"Come on," she told them, hurrying down an aisle. "They must have them somewhere. I always see them on TV."

"I don't know," Ashley said doubtfully. "Are these things good for your health?"

"They couldn't sell them on TV if they were bad for you," Christina argued.

"They sell hot dogs on TV, and you think *they're* bad for you," Katie reminded her.

"It's not the same." Christina just brushed off Katie's remark like so much dust.

"It's exactly the same!" Katie exploded.

"Well, this is different. I *want* to be *thin.*"

"You *are* thin," Ashley told her earnestly.

"Oh, yeah?" Christina challenged her. "Then why did Matt say I didn't look like a salad eater?"

"I don't know!" Ashley wailed. "There could have been a million reasons why he said that."

"It was probably a compliment," Katie said. "He meant you look like a real, down-to-earth, meat-eating person."

"In other words, I look beefy. *Fat.*"

"No!" Katie cried. "He meant you look healthy."

"I don't want to look healthy," Christina insisted.

"You don't?" Ashley asked with raised eyebrows.

Christina shook her head sulkily. "When someone says, 'You look healthy,' it's just another way of saying you look fat. It's like saying a girl has a good personality. You know what *that* means."

"That she's *ug-leee*," Katie supplied.

"Well, *healthy* is the same thing. It's code language for fat," said Christina.

"But Matt didn't say you look healthy," Ashley reminded her.

"See?" Christina said, meaningfully.

"See what?" Ashley asked.

"He doesn't think I look healthy. It's not healthy to be fat!" Christina shot back.

"Aaargh! Are you even listening to yourself?" Ashley yelped. "Christina, you have really lost your mind. You're not even making sense anymore. And you are absolutely not fat," she finished emphatically.

Christina shook her head stubbornly.

"Look," Katie said firmly. "If you were like Ruth Edwards at school, who weighs a ton and always has some kind of ice cream in her hand, I'd say, 'All right. You may have a point. Maybe you need to lose a few pounds.' Or if you were like Libby Jones, or Candy Martin, or Danny Mallo, or any of those really, really fat kids, I'd be encouraging you to lose weight. But you're not like them!" Katie shouted the last words.

"I could turn out like them if I don't watch out," Christina insisted.

Ashley rolled her green eyes to the ceiling. "I give up," she muttered. "You've lost your mind. I mean it."

Just then Christina found the diet aids section against the back wall of the pharmacy. "There are so many of them," she said despairingly. "How do I know which one will work for me?"

Ashley lifted a green box off a hook and began reading the back of it. "'Fat Away cuts appetite without nervousness.'" She looked at Christina and Katie. "Why would you be nervous?"

"You're nervous that you won't ever lose weight," Christina suggested.

"That's not it, Miss One-Track-Mind," Katie said impatiently. "I've heard some of these things can make you feel all jittery and nervous. They race your system or something."

"Oh," Christina said, embarrassed. "Well, I don't care. I can deal with that. Besides, it says here it doesn't do that."

She took the box from Ashley. "I'll take this one, since it won't make me nervous."

"Yeah, it's bad enough being insane without being nervous, too," Katie taunted.

"Ha, ha!" Christina said drily. "You're a riot. What's wrong with wanting to improve yourself?"

"Nothing," Katie said. "But girls get so crazy about their weight. It's really nuts. Besides, what do you need this dumb product for? If you want to lose weight, why not just eat less?"

"Because I get too hungry," Christina replied.

"How do you know? Have you ever dieted before?" Katie asked relentlessly.

"No, but I know I couldn't stand to not eat if I were hungry," Christina said.

"You couldn't stand it because it's normal to eat when you're hungry. I've never seen you binge out on cookies or cakes or sodas, Christina. It's the people who do *that* who need to go on diets, not someone like you, who eats normally," Katie told her. "This doesn't seem like your type of thing, either. I would expect you to meditate your way to thinness or to use crystal power to cut fat, or something like that. I mean, isn't there some *other* way?"

"I *am* going to meditate to increase my willpower," Christina said seriously. "I don't know about using crystals, but maybe there is a way I can figure out to do that, too. I'm going to do those things *plus* take these things. That way, one way or another, I'm sure to lose weight."

Katie sighed deeply. "You're a total lunatic, you know that?"

"I am not," Christina retorted.

"I don't think Christina is fat," Ashley said to Katie. "I understand how she feels, though. She isn't thin like girls on TV or in magazines. If she wants to be *that* thin, it's her business. And maybe she's right about the ballet. Maybe she *is* too heavy right now to be a ballet dancer. She's heavier than any ballerinas I've ever seen."

"Ballerinas look like skeletons to me," Katie grumbled. "You could blow them away just by sneezing."

"Ballet dancers happen to be extremely strong," Christina said. "I'd like to see you leap into the air like that."

"Well, I don't know how they do it when there's nothing to them," Katie muttered.

Christina studied Katie a moment. Their builds were very similar; they were both tall, broad-shouldered, and long-legged. Katie was more solid than Christina. She might not care, but Christina did.

She carried the box of Fat Away toward the cash register. Midway up the aisle, she stopped short.

"Oomph," Katie sputtered as she bumped into her.

Ashley crashed into the two of them. "What? What's the matter?"

"Matt's over by the cashier," Christina hissed, pointing toward the front of the store where Matt stood looking over a collection of magazines on a low shelf next to the cash register.

"Go talk to him," Ashley urged.

"What should I do with this?" Christina asked,

discreetly waving the Fat Away box. "I don't want *him* to know I'm on a diet!"

"Go put it back on the shelf," Katie advised.

Christina ran back down the aisle and returned the Fat Away to the shelf. Then she hurried back to her friends. "Hurry," Ashley said. "He just bought a magazine. I think he's leaving."

"Okay," Christina said resolutely. "Here I go."

She tossed her hair back and headed quickly up the aisle. She caught sight of him by the front door as he was just about to leave. "Matt!" she called. "Hi!"

Matt turned and smiled.

Christina's heart raced. What a gorgeous smile! And she loved the way his hair fell around his face. Something about him was so . . . so different from any boy she'd ever met. She'd never, ever met a boy who made her feel this way before.

"Hi, Christina," he said. "I just got the new *Science World*," he told her, lifting the magazine from its brown paper bag.

"Wow! You're interested in science?" Christina asked. Christina had always liked science well enough, but now it suddenly seemed like the most fascinating subject on earth.

"I know, I know. I sound like a geek, right?" Matt laughed.

"No, not at all," Christina assured him.

"What I really like is the paranormal stuff they cover," Matt said. "You know, like, ESP and stuff."

"You're into that?" Christina asked, more impressed than ever.

"Yeah. They cover all the research being done on that stuff. Every month they cover something different." He thumbed through the magazine. "Like, look at this. They have these super-cool examples of Kirlian photography, which shows the electromagnetic fields surrounding all living things."

"You mean auras," Christina said excitedly.

"Exactly," he said. Behind his wire-rim glasses his green eyes were wide with enthusiasm. "Not many people know about auras."

"Oh, I'm very interested in them," Christina said sincerely.

"Then, here, look at these." Matt showed her a photo of a leaf. The leaf was dark but surrounded by a glowing white border of light. Another photo showed a woman with the same kind of glow surrounding her. "These prove that everything gives off energy," he said.

"I sometimes think animals can see or sense auras," Christina said.

"You do?" Matt said. "I thought I was the only one who had goofy ideas like that."

Christina laughed. "No, I have them, too."

"You know what I wonder about sometimes," Matt said, stepping closer to Christina. "You know paintings of angels, where they have these beautiful halos? Well, I wonder if that's the artist's way of showing that angels are just brimming over with energy. You know, that they have these huge auras of amazing light."

"That makes so much sense," Christina said. And from what she'd experienced, it really did. The angels she'd seen gave off a terrific light. Sometimes it was nearly blinding. Other times—like the day she'd followed the angel in the woods—it was gentle and mesmerizing. "Do you believe in angels?" she asked Matt.

He shrugged self-consciously. "Yeah, I guess. I mean . . . I do, yeah."

"Me, too," Christina said. "In fact, I'm absolutely sure they exist."

She'd known there was something special about Matt. How many other boys believed in angels? Or, even if they did, how many would admit it? To a girl?

Christina admired the scientific approach he took to the subject. It was a very attractive trait. And it was so easy to talk to him. He would never laugh at the things she believed in.

They had so much in common. Maybe she *didn't* really need to lose weight. After all, when you were soulmates with someone, what did a few pounds matter?

"The reason I'm sure about angels is . . ." Christina began expansively, suddenly feeling the urge to tell Matt everything that was inside her.

Matt cut her off by gently laying one hand on her arm. His touch made Christina feel like a pleasant electricity was running through her.

"Christina, I'm sorry, but I have to go. I'm late meeting a friend."

"Oh," Christina said, trying to hide her disappointment. "Oh, sure. Sorry to keep you here, yakking away."

"Oh, no," he said, slipping his magazine back into the bag. "I'd like to talk some more. You're the only person I know who's interested. My friends all think this stuff is nutty, so it's great talking to someone who really understands, you know?"

"We should talk some more then," Christina said, emboldened by the connection she felt to him.

"Yeah, we should," he agreed, smiling. "I'll see you soon. Bye."

Christina lifted her hand to wave. "Bye."

The moment Matt was out the door, Katie and Ashley were upon her. "You guys were really smiling!" Ashley noted excitedly. "Things looked pretty cozy."

"He's interested in auras," Christina said blissfully.

Katie snickered, then sighed with comic happiness. "Ahhh, the perfect man. He's into auras. You two are made for each other."

"We are," Christina agreed, disregarding Katie's teasing tone. "Too bad he had to go meet someone."

Ashley went to the glass door of the pharmacy and looked out. "He's still standing on the corner," she observed. "I wonder who he's meeting."

"Whoever it is is even later than he was," Christina said.

"It's probably just Darrin or Mike or somebody like that," said Katie, without interest.

"No," Ashley reported in a strange voice. "It's not one of them."

Curious, Christina moved to the window. Katie was right behind her, looking over her shoulder.

Christina's jaw dropped when she saw who Matt was meeting.

"Molly Morgan!" Katie gasped.

Silently, they watched as Molly piled her shopping bags on the corner and wrapped Matt in a hug. She looked spectacular in a white crocheted sweater and skin-tight jeans. Her long white-blonde hair swung down to her waist as she hung on Matt's arm.

"What could he possibly see in *her*?" Ashley muttered.

"I guess she is one of the *friends* who doesn't understand about auras at all," Christina said unhappily.

"She doesn't understand about *anything* at all," Katie added.

"But look at her," Christina said enviously. "She's gorgeous."

"You're prettier than she is," Ashley said.

"Thanks," Christina replied. "But she's so thin. *So* thin."

All the happy enthusiasm Christina had felt about Matt just a moment ago drained out of her as if she were a balloon someone had untied. She turned away from the door.

She didn't stand a chance with a boy who believed in angels and auras—the most perfect boy on earth for her—all because she wasn't thin enough.

But what if she was thinner? Everything might change. She'd look like the other girls in the ballet. She might look even better.

And Matt might notice her as more than a friend. If he liked Molly, he obviously liked thin girls.

"Hey, where are you going?" Katie called after Christina as she headed toward the back of the pharmacy.

"To get that box of Fat Away," Christina told her. "Thin City, here I come!"

10

"Quiet," Christina softly scolded her growling stomach. That Saturday morning she'd eaten half a grapefruit and a Fat Away candy for breakfast. Even though the Fat Away was supposed to take away her appetite, her stomach obviously wanted more.

Christina was not about to give it more.

She sat cross-legged at the end of her bed, closed her eyes, and went back to her meditation. "Ohmmmmmmmmmmm," she hummed, letting the sound vibrate in her head. Christina had been meditating since she was seven. She loved the calm that came over her when she was able to completely clear all thoughts from her head and fill it with the long, drawn-out *ohm* sound.

Today she wasn't having an easy time of it. Pictures kept swimming through her head, pictures of food.

Steamy pancakes dripping butter and warm syrup. Rich, glistening sticky buns streaked with white icing.

"This isn't working," she said, opening her eyes. She'd hoped meditating would put her in a good mood. It often did. But since she'd started dieting and taking Fat Away three days before, she'd only felt crabby and tired.

Leaning back on her elbows, she gazed around her bedroom at the magazine pictures she'd taped to the wall for inspiration. They were pictures of thin models and thin ballerinas. In the middle of these was a black-and-white picture of Matt that she'd torn from the school paper. He was standing with the other winners of the science fair. He'd won third prize with his project on the Hubble Telescope.

"So cute," Christina sighed as she looked at his smiling face.

"Christina," her mother called from the hallway. "I'm going down to the stable. Want to come?"

"No, thanks," Christina called back.

Alice knocked and opened the bedroom door. "What are you doing today?"

"Exercising."

Her mother frowned. "Christina, I think you should take a break from all this exercise. Every time I look at you lately, you're exercising. What's going on?"

"I have a lot of catching up to do in ballet class," Christina said, telling half the truth. "I need to lose some weight."

"I don't know," Alice sighed. "You look fine to me."

"Not compared with the other girls, Mom. You should see them."

"Well, please don't overdo it. Did you eat breakfast?"

"I did," Christina told her.

"What did you eat?" her mother wanted to know.

"Grapefruit." Her mother didn't know about the Fat Away. Suspecting she might object, Christina had decided not to mention it to her.

"Eat something more, please," Alice requested firmly.

"I will," Christina told her.

When her mother left, Christina took a jump rope from her closet. She'd read a magazine article saying jumping rope was a great way to lose weight.

She took the rope outside and began to jump. A warm breeze blew. Above her, puffy clouds billowed in the clear, startlingly blue sky.

After jumping rope a while, Christina grew bored. It might be more fun and interesting to jog through the woods, she decided. Tossing the rope by the front door, she set off jogging toward the woods.

When she was in among the trees, Christina inhaled the deep, wet smell of the woods. She jogged past bushes with tender green leaves. In a patch of sunlight, she saw a shock of orange—tiger lilies bent gracefully on their long stalks.

Christina kept running, mindless of her direction. She always found it easy to lose track of the outside world when she was in the woods. Something about the place always induced a dreamy happiness in her.

Before long, she found herself at the top of the hill leading down to the Angels Crossing Bridge. The glistening creek beneath the bridge rushed noisily along, swelling with water from the previous week's rains.

After catching her breath, Christina jogged down to the bridge. Her feet clomped heavily on the boards as she jogged across.

On the other side, she stopped, panting, and gazed around. She decided to follow the creek to the right and see where it led.

Christina jogged along the water's edge for awhile, letting the lively sound of rushing water fill her head. At first, she felt great, exhilarated and free. Then, slowly, she became aware of a queasy feeling growing in the pit of her stomach.

Christina slowed to a walk. Her breathing had grown heavy. Her skin felt cold and clammy. Her stomach knotted into a sharp cramp.

Clutching her stomach, she staggered forward. The pain clouded her mind. All she knew was that it hurt. She couldn't believe how much.

Several feet ahead, the flat surface of a large boulder seemed to offer a place to rest. Christina stumbled toward it. She got there just as another cramp took hold of her.

"Owwwwww," she moaned, leaning on the rock. When would this stop? How was she going to get home?

"Somebody help me, please," she murmured, falling heavily against the boulder. "Please."

Suddenly her ears were filled with a sharp, explosive

crack, like gunfire. Something cylindrical and silver flew high above her head, then quickly arched back and curved toward the earth. Toward Christina.

There was no time to get away. Christina covered her head and waited for the silver object to hit her.

11

"Oh, my gosh, are you all right?"

From her crouched position, Christina heard the boy's voice. After a second's consideration, she realized she *was* all right. Whatever had been hurtling toward her hadn't hit her.

Taking her hands from her head, she slowly looked up into a pair of clear, blue eyes. "It's you!" Christina gasped.

It was the young man the angel had led Christina to a few days before. Up close, he looked younger than she'd thought, probably sixteen or seventeen at most.

"Of course, it's me," he said, his voice low and rich with the country twang found among families who'd lived in the woods and hills of Pine Ridge for generations. "What do you mean?"

Christina spotted the slingshot at his side and

cringed away from him in fear. As she did, she realized that her stomach no longer hurt. Her head even felt clearer, too. It was weird.

Had her fear choked her into wellness? she wondered.

The boy glanced down. "You don't have to be afraid of this. I was just shooting cans."

"Cans?" Christina questioned.

"Target-shooting. For fun," he explained. He nodded toward the dented silver can lying at Christina's feet. A rock had made a perfect crater in its center. It was the can that Christina had seen coming toward her.

A surge of hot anger raced through her. "You could have hit me!" Christina cried, realizing that it could easily have happened if she hadn't been behind the boulder. "Did you ever think of that?"

"Sorry," he said. "There's usually never anyone in this part of the woods." His eyes narrowed as he studied her face. "I've seen you before," he said slowly. "You were on a horse."

Christina nodded.

"What were you doing so deep in the woods?"

Christina wondered if she should tell him about the angel. It sounded so strange and she didn't know him at all. "I was just riding," she said.

"Why did you bolt away from me like that?" he asked.

"The slingshot," she explained. "It scared me. I hate weapons."

"Sometimes you need a weapon," the boy said with an off-handed shrug.

Christina got to her feet and brushed dirt off her jeans. "Funny, I was feeling sick, but the feeling passed," she told the boy. "I was running, and suddenly I just felt terrible."

"Running?"

"For exercise."

"Maybe you got hungry," he guessed. "Or dried out."

"Maybe."

"Want some lunch?" he offered.

Remembering her diet, Christina hesitated. Then she remembered the awful pain in her stomach. What if it came back? She knew she should probably eat something. "Lunch sounds good. I suppose I am pretty hungry," she said. "But where are we going to get food around here?"

"I brought some food." He walked to the other side of the rock and Christina followed him. Alongside a pile of empty cans was a crumpled brown paper grocery bag. The boy pulled out a long loaf of bread and a big hunk of white cheese. "Here," he said, breaking the bread in half.

Christina took the bread and cheese. She'd planned to have a salad for lunch that afternoon, but she was suddenly too ravenous to resist the food the boy offered. Filled with a fierce hunger, she began eating. She'd never tasted anything so delicious as the crusty bread and tangy cheese together.

"Whoa!" the boy laughed after a moment. "You really *were* hungry!"

Embarrassed, Christina realized she'd really been wolfing down the food. "I guess I was," she said sheepishly.

"What's your name?" asked the boy as he settled, cross-legged, on the ground and began eating, too.

"Christina. What's yours?"

"Adam."

"Do you live in that house I saw you by the other day?"

Adam shifted position. He looked around thoughtfully, as if he were deciding how to answer. "I come and I go," he said finally. "But that's my family, yeah."

When they finished eating, Adam stood. "I didn't bring anything to drink. Want to go back to the house to get something?"

"Okay," Christina agreed. She knew she probably shouldn't just go off with this guy. After all, she didn't know him, really. But, she reasoned, she'd already been to his house—kind of—once before. He *seemed* nice enough. Anyway, Christina had a good feeling about him. She could almost see his aura, clear and pure and kind. She stood up. "Let's go," she said.

He picked up his slingshot, and, together, they headed through the woods. The pines in this part of the woods were so thick and gnarled, so utterly other-worldly looking, that Christina could easily imagine all sorts of fairies, sprites, elves, and leprechauns living among them. She felt certain it was in shadowy, ancient woods like these that those kinds of fanciful stories originated.

The trees themselves almost seemed alive with some sort of mysterious, ancient life force.

They walked along side by side, talking little. The burbling sound of the rushing creek slowly receded until it was completely gone, and the air grew cooler, telling Christina they were walking deeper and deeper into the woods.

It seemed they were going farther than she remembered going the other day. But, of course, she'd been on horseback then.

Finally, they crested a hill. Below was the ramshackle building, just as Christina remembered it. Only today, a heavy-set gray-haired woman hung clothing on a line strung between two trees. Two young girls hung on the tire swing, and three boys chased one another in the space between the tree and the house.

"Come on," Adam said. Christina followed him down the hill. When they were almost there, the woman looked up warily. The two girls ran and hid behind her. The boys froze where they were.

Despite the wave of shyness washing over her, Christina forced a friendly smile to her lips. "Wait here," Adam said when they reached the yard. "I'll go get us something to drink."

As Adam headed for the house, one after another, he playfully ruffled the blond hair of the towheaded boys, who stood frozen, still staring at Christina. The tallest boy looked up at Adam with a questioning expression but didn't speak.

"Hi, there," said the gray-haired woman, stepping toward Christina. Her voice was rich with the same country inflections as Adam's. "Can I do something for you?"

"No, thanks," Christina replied pleasantly.

The woman's gray-blue eyes narrowed as she drew closer to Christina. Despite the gray in her long, dark hair and the lines in her face, there was liveliness in her eyes and energy in her walk that made it hard to tell how old she really was. "What brings you to these parts, then?" she asked, lightly.

"I was jogging, and I suddenly didn't feel very well," Christina began.

The woman's wary demeanor was instantly replaced with an expression of concern. Before Christina could say more, the woman was by her side with her hand tucked under Christina's elbow.

"Well, come right here, dear," she said kindly, guiding Christina to the wide, smooth stump of a cut-down tree. "Sit. What can I get you?"

"Thanks, but I'm fine now. I just need something to drink and I'll—"

The woman turned to one of the blond boys. "Jeb. Pump us some water here, please."

"That's all right," Christina said.

She was about to explain that Adam was coming out with drinks when the tallest boy came to her side with a ladle of water. "Drink that, hon," said the woman, handing her the ladle. "You'll feel better."

The icy cold water felt wonderful going down. "Thanks," she said, handing the ladle back to Jeb. The boy smiled shyly at her and then ran off.

The two girls joined them. They seemed to be about three and six. Both had wavy, waist-length brown hair. "These are Mariah and Melody," the woman introduced the girls.

"Hi." Christina smiled at them. "I'm Christina."

The older girl smiled, revealing two missing teeth on top. "That's my favorite name," she lisped.

"Thanks," said Christina. "Melody is a pretty name, too."

The girl beamed.

"So is Mariah," Christina added quickly, not wanting to slight the younger girl.

"Want to see our room?" Mariah offered eagerly.

Christina looked to the woman for approval of this suggestion.

"It's fine with me, if you want to," she said with a bemused grin. "But maybe you ought to just rest here awhile."

"Thank you, but I'll be fine," Christina told her.

"Come on," Melody said, taking Christina's hand.

Christina let the little girls lead her into the house. Inside, it was shadowy and cool. The sunlight filtered in through yellowed, half-drawn shades, giving the room a golden glow.

As Mariah led her through the house, Christina was reminded of the soft, golden light in photographs of her grandmother when she was a girl. The furniture was worn and old-fashioned. Faded wallpaper in a pattern of small blue flowers was yellowed and peeling at the seams.

She'd expected to see Adam there inside the house, but saw no sign of him. "Do you know where Adam is?" she asked Mariah.

"In the Garden of Eden," Mariah replied.

"Not that Adam, your brother."

Melody scowled gently. "We don't have a brother named Adam."

"What is he, then? Your cousin?" Christina asked.

"I don't know," Melody said with a shrug.

"His girlfriend is Eve," Mariah offered.

"No, I'm talking about the other Adam," Christina explained.

"Oh," said Mariah. "Well, we don't know where the other Adam is."

The girls led Christina up a short flight of wooden stairs. On the second floor the ceiling was low, reminding Christina of a kids' tree house. The girls' room was small, with a plain wooden bunk bed against one wall and two tall dressers against the other. Each bed was imperfectly made, as if by a child. A small table sat under the window, which opened out onto the yard.

On each pillow sat a handmade rag doll in a gingham dress; long, black-yarn hair; and shiny button eyes. Christina noticed that the only other toy in evidence was a wooden chess set on the small table.

The wooden chess pieces were carved into the shape of angels.

Christina picked up one of the larger pieces and turned it over in her hand. The exquisitely detailed carved angel gleamed with a silky smoothness. "Our Mom made that," Melody said proudly. "She's a carver."

Mariah pointed to the chess set. "See, the angels with the upturned wings play against the angels with the downturned wings."

"Our Mom loves angels," added Mariah. "She's always carving them. She carves other things, too, but she likes angels a lot."

"Who taught you to play chess?" Christina asked.

"Jeb," Melody replied. "Our dad taught him, but he's dead now. Jeb taught the rest of us."

"Jeb and Mom teach us everything," Mariah added.

"We don't go to school," Melody told Christina proudly.

"You don't?" Christina asked, confused.

The girls shook their heads. "No," Melody said. "Mom says she'd rather teach us."

Christina was suddenly filled with concern. Why weren't these children going to school like regular kids? Was that even legal?

Christina was anxious to ask Adam about this. He must be looking for her by now, anyway. "I'd better go find Adam," she told the girls.

"Is Adam your friend?" Mariah asked.

"Yes, I guess so," Christina replied. "Well, I'd better go find him. Bye."

"Bye," the girls said in one voice.

Making her way back down the stairs and through the shady house, Christina squinted when she stepped back out into the sunshine. She looked around to see where everyone was and spotted the woman sitting under a thick pine facing her sons.

By the woman's side Christina recognized an abacus, a traditional Chinese device used for counting. The woman slid the round pegs up and down the spindles of the abacus as she spoke to the boys. Christina realized they were in the middle of a math lesson and decided not to interrupt.

She walked around to the side of the house, looking for Adam. She found him sitting at a picnic table with a pitcher of lemonade and two glasses.

"Where'd you go to?" he asked pleasantly.

"I was visiting with Mariah and Melody," she said, sitting beside him. "They're sweet."

"Real sweet," he agreed as he handed her a glass of lemonade.

Christina took a sip and marveled at the delicious flavor, a combination of tart lemons and soothing sweetness. "Wow! This is great lemonade," she said. "What's in it?"

Adam smiled. "Honey. Karen keeps a beehive. It's out a ways in the woods, though."

"Is Karen the mother?" Christina asked.

"Yes," Adam said, nodding. "Her husband died right before Mariah was born. She's had a hard time supporting the family all by herself."

"She does beautiful carving," Christina said.

"I know," Adam said, nodding. "Her grandfather taught her to whittle when she was a girl. And she's been carving wood ever since."

"Why does Karen stay out here in the middle of nowhere?"

"She likes it," Adam said with a shrug. "Loves it, really. She and her husband grew up in the hills around here."

"Is it true the kids don't go to school?" Christina asked him.

"Well, they're home-schooled. Karen has to take them to the city every so often to have them tested. You know, to make sure she's teaching them enough and that they know what all kids their ages should know," Adam told her. His eyes lit with laughter. "Those kids go right off the chart!" he chuckled. "They ace every test they give them."

"Karen must be a good teacher, then," Christina said, though she still couldn't get over the feeling that they should be in school. "Don't they get lonely out here?" she asked.

"They've got each other," Adam said. "When they get older, I suppose they'll want to see more of the world. But right now they have a real good life here. They're going to grow up to be fine, straightforward people."

"You keep saying 'they,'" Christina pointed out. "What about you? Where do you fit in?"

"Oh, I'm just kind of a close relation," Adam said,

sliding off the bench. "Come on, I'll walk you back to the bridge so you won't get lost."

Christina followed him out of the yard, waving to Karen and the boys as they went. Karen got to her feet. "Do you feel all right, hon?" she called.

"Fine!" Christina called back. "Thank you!"

"You're welcome. Come see us again!"

Christina waved again and then continued up the hill with Adam. Looking back one last time, she felt as if she were leaving some magical spot that had somehow gotten stuck in time. She was surprised at how sad she felt to be leaving.

12

Christina and Ashley climbed the stairs to the dance studio together the next day. "You really don't have to come to class with me," Christina told Ashley for the hundredth time.

"I told you, I want to see these 'graceful swans' who are forcing you to starve yourself into a skeleton," Ashley said calmly.

Christina pounded one outer thigh. "I'm hardly a skeleton."

"Well, I'm worried about you, Christina," Ashley responded. "I never see you eating anything but Fat Away anymore."

"I *do* eat," Christina insisted. "I just don't eat like a hog, the way I used to."

"You never ate like a hog," Ashley disagreed. "Anyway, I'm curious about the class. Okay?"

"Okay," Christina mumbled. Ashley had begun acting like a worried mother hen, and it was getting annoying. This diet was just a simple bit of self-improvement. Christina didn't see why Ashley was making such a big deal over it.

"So, tell me more about this guy," Ashley said, changing the subject. "Was he cuter than Matt?"

Christina cocked her head and considered the question. "Not 'cuter than,' but just as cute. In a very different way, though."

"In what way different?" Ashley pressed.

"Hmmmm," Christina said as she thought. "Matt is brainy and sort of shy. Adam is like an outdoors person, more of a nature type."

"He knew about the Angels Crossing Bridge," Ashley said as they reached the top landing. "Did you ask him about angels? Had he ever seen any?"

"I didn't ask," Christina replied. "I didn't know how to begin."

"I suppose it *is* an odd topic of conversation."

"I could talk to Matt about angels, though," Christina said, remembering their conversation in the pharmacy.

"But you didn't tell him you'd actually seen them," Ashley reminded her.

"No," Christina admitted. "I didn't."

As they entered the studio, Molly walked by, already dressed in her black leotard and pink tights. She glanced disdainfully at Ashley and Christina and kept walking.

"What a snot," Ashley muttered.

"But I sure wish I had her figure," Christina sighed.

"I think she's *too* thin," Ashley commented. "She looks all right with her clothes on, but she looks so bony in that leotard."

"I'd rather be bony than fat," Christina insisted.

"You're impossible," Ashley countered, shaking her head.

Ashley waited while Christina changed into her dance outfit. "You can watch through the glass window in the waiting room," Christina told her.

Ashley headed for the waiting room while Christina hurried into class. It was weird. All week Christina had been feeling really good about herself. Her diet seemed to be working. She'd only lost about four pounds, but she *felt* better. It sounded corny, but she actually felt lighter, as though she could effortlessly soar through the air and land with the soft touch of a butterfly.

Now, in the long-mirrored classroom, Christina's airy limbs grew heavier with each step as the mirrors shot back image after image of a Christina who was—still—visibly larger than the slender girls whose perfect reflections seemed to mock her everywhere she looked. Just the previous night she'd pirouetted this way and that before the mirror at home. Then her image was tall and graceful, her arms and legs willowy, the effect of her diet totally obvious.

Deep in her heart of hearts, Christina knew she wasn't really fat. She'd always felt good about herself before. Resolutely she pushed those thoughts away. The only reason she'd felt good before was because she'd been sadly deluded. She'd been hiding from the truth, she told herself fiercely. The truth was what she could see in these awful mirrors: she was fat, fat, fat. This week she'd eat less and exercise even more. She was determined to make this work.

Just then Amy, her teacher, glided gracefully into the room. "From now on, girls, we're going to get really serious about rehearsing for the recital," she announced. "The end of August will be here sooner than you think."

She instructed the girls to choose partners. Christina looked around helplessly as the girls scrambled to partner with their friends. When they were done, of course, Christina was the odd girl out. There was no one left to be her partner.

Amy frowned thoughtfully. Then she walked over to where Molly stood with another girl, a girl she seemed pretty friendly with named Lisa. "Christina, come here and be partners with Lisa," she instructed.

"Hey, that's not fair," Molly muttered rebelliously.

"Molly, I'll want you to dance a solo," Amy explained.

The sour expression melted from Molly's face. "Oh . . . well, okay," she said, obviously flattered.

Perfect Molly, thought Christina. *Captain of the cheerleaders. Soloist at the dance recital. Matt's girlfriend. Skinny as a rail.*

Maybe all these things came to her *because* she *was* so thin. The world probably just fell into place for very thin girls. Everything came to them easily because they were so thin and attractive.

I'll be that thin soon, too, Christina told herself, determined to think positively. All she'd had for breakfast were two pieces of dry toast. At lunch she'd had only a diet soda.

Christina glanced at Molly in the mirror. Maybe Molly *was* a little bony, but being bony was what made her look like a fashion model.

Amy turned on the classical music, and Christina straightened to attention.

With calm confidence the teacher guided the girls through the choreography. Christina tried to give it her complete concentration, but her body just wouldn't cooperate.

It seemed her legs couldn't keep up with the count. Her brain couldn't seem to register the right and left changes quickly enough. She was always a beat or two behind the other dancers.

"Front, one, two, three, and now back, one, two, three," Amy put them through their paces. "Come on, Christina, keep up," Amy urged her.

Christina tried. She visualized the graceful ballerinas she'd seen in *Swan Lake*. Their feet flew across the dance floor as if cushioned and lifted by a current of air beneath them. Why wouldn't her feet do the same?

She pushed herself to feel the music, to let it move her. But it didn't. Her feet felt leaden, her arms awkward.

"Ow!" Lisa griped as Christina stepped on her foot.

"Sorry," Christina muttered apologetically.

"*Échappé*, right!" Amy instructed, using the French term for a small jump.

Christina went left.

Suddenly a terrible cracking sound—and a worse pain—filled her head. She clutched her forehead to make the hot anguish subside.

"Aaaahhh!" Beside her, Lisa shrieked in pain.

Christina realized they'd collided and banged heads. She squeezed her head with both hands and ground her molars in her effort to control the pain. It was hard to believe that a stupid thing like hitting heads with another person could hurt so much.

"You oaf!" Lisa yelled, pink with pain. She, too, clutched her forehead. "She said *right*, not *left*, you idiot!"

Christina sensed something warm and coppery-tasting on her lips. Wiping her mouth, she saw it was blood. She'd bitten her lip when they'd crashed into one another.

"Are you all right?" Amy asked as the classical music played on in the background. The whole class had stopped dancing, and everyone was watching.

"She doesn't belong in this class," Lisa sobbed, still clutching her head as tears ran down her cheeks. "If she's my partner, I'm going to look like an idiot!"

Molly came over and put her arm around Lisa. "Thank goodness she didn't trip you and break your leg," she said in a voice loud enough for the entire class to hear.

"Come to my office and let's see about that lip," Amy suggested to Christina. "Molly, sit with Lisa. I'll be right back. Class, take a break."

Mortified, Christina followed Amy out of the studio. Ashley came out of the waiting room. "How do you feel?" she asked.

"Terrible," Christina muttered.

"Come into my office, Christina," Amy said, opening the glass door to her office just off the studio.

"I'll wait right here," Ashley told her, frowning worriedly.

Inside her office Amy opened a small refrigerator and took out a cold pack. "Hold this to your lip," she advised, handing Christina the pack. "Rest on my couch."

Christina put the pack on her lip and sat on the blue velvet couch. Amy sat at her desk chair. "Christina, I'm afraid I've done you a terrible disservice," she began after a moment. "I should never have let you sign up for these classes."

"What do you mean?" Christina asked, beginning to feel panicky. Was she being thrown out of class?

"You're a beginner, and in the next few weeks I'm going to be too involved in preparing for the recital to work individually with you. And you need individual work, Christina."

Christina sat forward anxiously. "But, but . . . I can catch up."

"I don't think so, Christina. It's just too much to ask. A lot of these girls have been dancing for five years or even longer. It's not fair to ask you to keep up with them. What I suggest is that you quit for now. I'll refund your money completely. Then, if you want, start again in September, when the class is just beginning. I'll have more time then to work with you."

To her great embarrassment, tears ran down Christina's face. "I'm sorry," she apologized, roughly brushing them away.

"No, Christina, *I'm* sorry," Amy said, handing her a tissue. "This is simply a bad time of year to come into a class with no previous experience."

"I'll work really hard," Christina said, desperate to stay in the class. "I'm sorry about what happened. I'll be more careful next time. It won't happen again, I—"

"It's not that," Amy said. "It's not your fault, Christina. You can't be expected to know as much as the girls who've been studying so much longer. The recital is very important to the girls, and we have put all our attention toward it. I should have thought more about that when I let you sign up. I *am* sorry. I know how much this means to you, and I feel I've let you down."

Staring dismally down at her ballet slippers, Christina nodded dumbly. She could tell Amy's mind was made up. There was no use arguing or pleading.

Amy wrote out a check and handed it to her. "Here's your refund, Christina. Please try to understand, and just be patient for a while longer. I'm truly sorry about this."

Taking her check, Christina stood up.

"How do you feel?" Amy asked.

"All right," Christina lied. Her head and lip ached terribly. But much worse than that, she felt humiliated, and depressed, and utterly crushed. Her dream had turned into a nightmare of failure and defeat.

Amy put her hand on her shoulder. "I'll look forward to seeing you in September."

Christina nodded. She didn't think Amy really wanted her back. And, even if she did, Christina didn't think she could face coming back, *ever.* Not after this.

She'd never been asked to leave anything in her life. It was such a disgrace. With her head down and her eyes hot with unshed tears, Christina started for the door.

"Christina," Amy said, just as Christina was about to leave.

"Yes?" Christina replied, her hand on the doorknob.

"Do you know what you want from this dance class?"

"To learn to dance," Christina replied in bewilderment. What else could she possible want?

"I mean, do you want to dance for enjoyment or do you want to make a career out of it?"

"Oh, a career," Christina answered quickly. *Would this make a difference to Amy?* she wondered hopefully. Would Amy now see she was serious and reconsider asking her to leave?

Amy sat back in her chair and bit her lip anxiously. Then she sat forward and folded her hands on her desk.

"Christina, with work you can make a lot of progress. You could even become a very good dancer. But I really feel I must tell you that . . ." Here she paused a minute. "Well, it's that the bodies of classical dancers usually conform to a certain body type. Christina, I can see that you don't have the shape for a classical dancing *career.*"

"You mean ballerinas are thin and I'm not," Christina said with grim bluntness.

"No," Amy said quickly. "Well, I mean, it's true ballerinas are thin. But that's not the only thing I meant. You're a slim enough girl but you're also quite tall and broad shouldered. Most corps ballet dancers are very strong but not as athletically built as you are and to even become a prima ballerina, most dancers must be in the corps first."

"Core?" Christina questioned.

"Corps, c-o-r-p-s," Amy explained. "The *corps de ballet*, the background dancers. Classical dancers even have a certain proportion of head size to body size which you don't have."

The tears finally welled and spilled over in Christina's eyes. Embarrassed, she roughly wiped her eyes. "So, you're saying I should forget it."

"Well," Amy said with an unhappy sigh. "Maybe a career as a classical ballerina might not be for you, but there are other forms of dance which might be more suited to your particular—"

Christina couldn't listen anymore. More tears were about to rush forward and she couldn't bear the humiliation of standing there crying. She rushed from the office, tucking her head as far down as possible.

Although she refused to look their way, Christina could feel the eyes of the other girls on her. They must all be staring at her, she thought. They must be pitying her or thinking how ridiculous she was.

Lifting her head a bit, Christina saw Ashley waiting outside in the hallway, leaning against the wall. "Are you okay?" Ashley asked anxiously.

"I've been kicked out of class," Christina said, a fresh rush of tears springing to her eyes. "And Amy thinks I should forget about ever becoming a ballerina."

Ashley was aghast. "Just because of one accident?"

"No," Christina sobbed. "Because I'm a fat, clumsy moose!"

13

"Please cheer up," Katie begged Christina. "I can't stand seeing you like this."

Ashley, Katie, and Christina were wandering through the Pine Ridge Mall. It was the day after the ballet class. *The ballet disaster*, as Christina now thought of it. Christina had agreed to come out just to make her friends stop nagging her, although she really would rather have remained in her room, feeling sorry for herself.

"Let's go get milk shakes," Ashley suggested. "That will cheer you up."

Christina smiled cynically. "Oh, that's sneaky, Ashley, but not too subtle. You can't trick me into eating *that* easily."

"Well, you have to start eating," Ashley said, folding her arms in a surprisingly no-nonsense gesture for the usually easygoing Ashley. "That's all there is to it."

"Yeah, I agree," Katie said. "Maybe you should be consulting your horoscope about this, or the tarot cards or something!"

"I can't believe *you* are saying that," Christina cried in amazement. "You, the supposedly hard-headed, sensible one. You, the total cynic!"

"I'm desperate," Katie told her. "I've never seen you so down before."

Christina appreciated Katie's concern, but she didn't feel like being cheered up. She was down in the dumps, and she felt like staying there right now. After all, didn't she have an awful lot to be upset over?

"I'll be all right," Christina said. "Everyone's allowed to get bummed out once in awhile, aren't they?"

"I suppose," Katie conceded. "But that's why you have friends—to cheer you up."

Suddenly Katie grabbed hold of Christina's arm and tugged her into the doorway of a music store. "Are you going nuts?" Christina asked her. "What did you do that for?"

"No, I'm not nuts. I just wanted to show you . . . uh . . . this CD," Katie replied nervously.

Ashley ducked into the doorway with them, checking quickly over her shoulder. Looking past Ashley, Christina saw what she was looking at.

Molly and Matt were walking hand in hand through the mall.

"It's okay," Christina told her friends. "I see them. I can handle it."

She gazed at Matt. He was so sweet and cute. What was he doing with that witch Molly anyway? Was it just because he liked her looks? Was he that shallow? He didn't seem to be, but maybe he was.

"I'll never understand boys," Ashley sighed, as though she'd been reading Christina's mind.

The three girls continued watching as Matt and Molly passed by. "I swear, she looks skinnier every time I see her," Katie observed.

"Lucky her," Christina said gloomily.

"I don't think so. If you ask me, she looks gross," Ashley said emphatically. "She's *too* thin."

Christina let out a morose sigh. "You know what they say, you can't be too rich or too thin."

"*They*—whoever *they* are—are wrong," Ashley insisted confidently.

"Matt and Molly don't exactly look like the perfect, happy couple," Katie pointed out. "Did you see the looks on their faces?"

Christina had to admit they'd looked pretty glum.

"Anyway, forget about Matt and Molly," Katie said brightly. "Let's talk about something more interesting. Ashley told me about Adam, the new guy you met."

"I don't even know if I'll ever see him again," Christina said. "Besides, I still like Matt a lot."

"Forget Matt," Katie said. "I want to hear about Adam. He sounds cool."

"Way cool," Ashley agreed. "Go on, Christina, tell her."

As Christina told Katie about Adam and the family in the woods, an enthusiastic smile swept across Katie's face. "He's *obviously* the one for you," Katie said, as if it were all perfectly clear. "An angel led you to him, right?"

"I know, but . . ." Christina still wasn't sure why. Angels didn't really care about people's love lives, did they? Didn't they have more important things to do? Christina wondered for the first time if the angel hadn't really been trying to help Karen, not her. Was there something Christina needed to do for the family?

Christina thought about the angels they'd met, Edwina, Norma, and Ned. Were they still nearby? Maybe if she went to the bridge, she could find them. Maybe they'd know what to do about Karen and her kids. And about Adam.

Silently, Christina decided to do that. She wasn't sure if she'd be able to contact them, but it had to be worth a try.

The girls left the music store and continued meandering through the mall. The more Christina thought about it, the more it seemed to her there must be some reason she'd been led to Karen and the children. But what was it?

"Can we go home now?" Christina asked plaintively at last. "I'm just not in the mood to hang out."

"All right," Ashley agreed reluctantly. "Let's go out and get the bus."

They rode the bus home without much conversation. Christina couldn't stop thinking about Karen and the kids. She thought about Adam, too. She liked him a lot. He was really nice, and she felt so comfortable with him. He seemed like the big brother she'd always wished she had.

Do I have a crush on him? she asked herself.

No. She didn't think so. He didn't make her heart pound the way Matt did.

But liking Matt was a lost cause. Matt was with Molly. Any interest Christina thought he'd had in her must have been her imagination—the same stupid imagination that had led her to believe she could actually become a ballerina. She slumped into her bus seat and stared blankly out the window until the low stores of Pine Ridge gave way to the tree-lined road that wound toward the ranch.

Not long after that came Katie's stop. "See you tomorrow," she said with a wave as she got off.

About five stops later, Christina and Ashley got off right by the ranch. They walked down the dirt road that cut through a rolling pasture of grazing horses. "Want to come to my house?" Ashley offered.

"No, thanks," Christina said as they walked past her own small house. "I think I'll go see if Mom's in the stable."

Champ, Ashley's golden retriever, trotted off the porch to meet her. Scratching him between the ears, Ashley led him back to her neat, picture-pretty house across from the stable. "Feel better, Christina," Ashley called from the porch.

"Thanks," Christina replied as she headed across the driveway.

Inside the stable she found her mother brushing Bridey. "Why so glum, chum?" Alice asked, giving Christina a calm, searching look.

Christina shrugged. "I got kicked out of ballet class, the boy I like likes someone else, and I'm a fat pig. Isn't that enough to make anyone bummed out?"

Her mother stopped brushing and leaned against the door to Bridey's stall. "Christina, I'm worried that all this dieting you're doing is getting to you."

"What do you mean, 'getting to me'?" Christina asked defensively.

"You haven't been yourself. You're gloomy, and you seem tired all the time."

Christina felt a deep irritation rise up in her. Why wouldn't everyone leave her alone? "I told you what was the matter," she snapped. "It's not the diet! The diet's about the only positive thing I'm doing right now! Can't you take my problems seriously?"

"Christina, I'm sorry you're upset," Alice replied levelly. "I *do* take your problems seriously. At least, I take your feelings seriously. But because I've lived longer, I also see the bigger picture. You can start ballet again in September. I also know that although you're hurting now, in time you'll find another boy you like just as well, maybe even better. Trust me. That's how it works."

"You don't understand at all," Christina exploded. "By

then I'll be *way* too old to start ballet. And I won't find another boy like Matt. Not ever!"

"You will, Christina."

"*You* didn't find anyone else after Dad left," Christina said harshly.

Even as the words tumbled from her lips, she didn't understand why she was being so cruel or why she felt so angry.

Her mother looked at her, speechless for a moment.

"I'm sorry," Christina mumbled, suddenly awash in remorse.

"You're right, Christina," her mother said slowly. "I haven't found anyone to replace your father. But maybe I will someday. I keep hoping to. And that's the way you have to feel, too."

Christina turned her back on her mother. "How can I *make* myself feel a certain way? I can only feel the way I feel!"

"And you feel really bad about yourself right now, don't you?" Alice said softly.

Without looking at her mother, Christina nodded. It was true. She felt fat and clumsy, stupid and unlovable—as she never had before. She wasn't sure where these feelings were coming from.

"Christina, sweetie, you're a lovely girl with so much to—"

Christina raised her hand. "Don't bother, Mom. It won't help."

Coming out of the stall, Alice put her arm around

Christina's shoulders. "You've always been so bright and enthusiastic about things. I can't stand to see you so—"

"That's when I was a kid, Mom. I'm not a kid anymore," Christina said, pulling away from her mother.

Alice sighed deeply. "Did you eat lunch?"

Whirling around, Christina faced her mother. "No! And I'm not going to! Why does everyone care so much if I eat or not?"

"Because we care about *you*!" her mother yelled back in exasperation.

"Well, don't waste your time!" Christina shouted. Blinded by her own tears, she tore out of the barn.

"Christina!" she heard her mother call from the doorway.

She didn't stop running.

Christina ran into the woods. She needed to escape from everyone. She needed to escape from herself.

14

Panting, Christina finally slowed to a walk only when she'd reached the Angels Crossing Bridge. She walked slowly toward the middle. She leaned hard against the railing and gazed down at the rushing water below.

Staring at the sparkling, spraying water as it leaped over rocks and swirled around branches, she let the steady, burbling sound of it lull her into a sort of trance—a place where her mind was at rest, free of all thought.

A board creaked.

Christina looked up sharply and gasped.

It was Adam.

"You startled me," Christina said, holding her hand over her pounding heart.

"Sorry," he said with a soft smile. He leaned on the railing beside her and gazed down at the water. "It's nice here, isn't it?" he said. "I find the sound of the water very soothing. What are you doing here?"

"I came here to think, I guess," Christina replied. She studied his handsome face and wondered why she didn't have a huge crush on him. He was certainly gorgeous, probably more perfectly handsome than Matt. Instead, she simply liked him—liked him a lot.

"What are you thinking about?" he asked.

"I was kicked out of ballet class," she said, too embarrassed to tell him the rest—about Matt, or about how she hated her looks. "I guess I'm trying to sort out how I feel about that, and other stuff, too."

"What happened at ballet class?" Adam asked.

"I wasn't good enough," she told him. "I started late, and the teacher didn't have enough time to help me catch up."

Funny, she thought. When she told the story it sounded so simple, so straightforward. She wasn't to blame. It wasn't because she was some awful klutz.

"That's too bad. Have you wanted to be a ballerina all your life?" he asked sympathetically.

Up until that moment, Christina thought she had.

"No," she answered, surprised by her own words. "It was something I always thought about and imagined doing. But it was only recently that I really wanted to be a dancer." She looked at his concerned face and decided to reveal a little more. "I thought it would make me more like an angel."

As soon as she spoke the words, they sounded foolish to her. She laughed self-consciously and looked away from him in embarrassment. "I suppose that sounds pretty crazy. But, you see, I've had angels on my mind lately."

"You have?" Adam asked, his blue eyes widening with interest.

Christina nodded and leaned closer. "I've seen angels," she confided. "I know they're real."

She waited for his reaction, expecting him to be surprised or doubtful.

"So have I," he said simply.

It was Christina who felt surprised. "You have?" she cried excitedly. "Where? Oh, how dense could I be? Here! Of course!" She laughed. "Right here on the bridge, of course!"

"This is a good place," he said. "It has a good feeling to it."

"I just knew it!" Christina cried. "That's what I think, too. It's a power spot, isn't it?"

"If that's what you call it," Adam agreed. "I guess you could say that."

"Do you remember the first day I saw you?" she asked, the words gushing forth enthusiastically. "An angel led me to you."

Adam smiled. "Really?"

"Yes. I don't know why. I still don't. But it was a dazzling, golden angel, surrounded by light. It was *so* beautiful, and it led me right to Karen's house. Can you think of any reason why?"

"I don't know. Angels are puzzling beings," Adam said, shaking his head. "But, speaking of Karen and the kids, would you like to come back with me and see them? I think Karen's cooking something special on the grill."

"Well . . . I'm on a diet." Christina hesitated.

Adam stepped back and studied her. "What are you dieting for?"

Christina blushed. "You don't think I need to diet?"

"Not at all," he said. "You look wonderfully healthy to me."

"Healthy?" Christina questioned skeptically.

"Beautiful," he said seriously.

There was no way Christina could stop her blush from burning redder. No boy had ever told her she was beautiful before. And somehow his words made her feel more beautiful than she could ever have imagined feeling.

"Want to come to Karen's?" he asked.

"I suppose I don't have to eat very much," Christina answered. "I *would* like to see Mariah and Melody again."

He held out his hand to her. "Come on."

She took his hand, amazed at its warmth and strong, firm grasp.

Maybe she shouldn't be holding hands with a boy she wasn't in love with. But, holding his hand felt so natural, so right. *A friendly hand-holding*, she thought, *not a romantic one.*

As they walked together through the woods, Christina noticed golden shards of light filtering down here and there through the thick pines. She figured it must be a little after five o'clock. There were only a few hours of daylight left. "I can't stay too long," she told Adam. "I don't know if I could find my way back in the dark."

"Okay," he agreed.

When they reached Karen's yard, Christina heard music. Peering down the hill she saw Karen standing in the yard playing the fiddle. The children swung each other, or spun in circles. The late afternoon breeze carried the delicious smell of something cooking on an outdoor grill.

Karen stopped fiddling as Christina and Adam approached. "Hi, there," she said, her face flushed with pleasure. "You're just in time to eat with us."

Karen and the children walked over to the grill. "I'll get you a plate!" Mariah cried, clearly excited to see Christina again.

"Wow! This looks great," Christina said, taking the plate from Mariah. "What is it?"

"Wild turkey," Karen replied. "The woods are full of them, if you know where to look. They taste a little gamy, but I've let this one sit in oil with some herbs, and that usually helps the flavor a lot."

Christina remembered Adam's slingshot. Now she understood why he had it. He'd been hunting for the family's food.

Normally, Christina didn't think much of hunters. Killing a live animal for fun seemed so cruel. But Adam wasn't killing for fun. The family needed to eat.

"Help yourself," Karen said.

"Thanks," Christina said, "but I don't eat meat, and besides, I'm on a diet."

"I can respect someone not eating meat," Karen said. "But you don't need to be on a diet. That's just crazy!"

Christina smiled. "That's what Adam said."

"Then listen to Adam, for heaven's sake," Karen said as she speared a dark-roasted potato from the coals with a long fork. "At least have a potato and some greens."

"Have some," Adam encouraged her. "Karen's a great cook."

"Eat up, everybody," Karen commanded happily.

Christina cut open her steaming potato and slathered it with some of the butter Karen had set out. She helped herself from a pot of string beans keeping warm on the grill and then dished up some fresh salad from the bowl on the table.

Adam had been sitting among the kids, eating. Holding his plate, he got up and joined her. "These string beans are great," Christina told him. "Normally, I don't even like string beans."

"Karen really knows how to season things," Adam agreed.

When everyone was finished eating, Christina helped clean up. Then Karen picked up her fiddle again.

She played a lively, country-style song. "Do you like bluegrass music?" Adam asked Christina.

"*What* kind of music?" she asked.

"Bluegrass," he said with a smile. "The Tennessee mountain people are famous for it. Karen's mom was from there. She taught Karen how to play."

The children had started dancing again. With arms and legs flying, their movements seemed perfectly suited to the fast-paced music, though Christina didn't recognize any of their steps as being from any kind of formal dance training. They were simply moving and having a wonderful time doing it.

Adam offered his hand to Christina. "Want to dance?"

"Pul-lease," she said, shaking her head. "I'm a terrible dancer. I just finished learning *that* the hard way."

"No, you're not," Adam disagreed. "Maybe you're just not a ballet dancer."

"That's for sure," Christina said with a self-deprecating laugh.

"Come on, dance with me," Adam coaxed. "I'll show you how."

Christina realized she was feeling good at that moment—full of good food and surrounded by nice people who wouldn't judge her harshly. "All right," she said, taking Adam's warm, strong hand.

Adam drew her closer to the others. Keeping hold of one of her hands, he raised his other hand in the air. With a small kick into the air, he began to dance. His booted feet flew across the grass in a dance that reminded Christina of an Irish jig yet was somehow different. It had a character all its own.

She swayed in place, studying his feet. Gradually, she picked up on certain patterns in the footwork.

"Come on, you try," he urged, smiling.

By then, the music felt as if it had gotten inside

Christina. She could no longer resist the urge to move. It was almost as if her feet had a life of their own as they began to kick and spin along the grass.

Adam danced along with her, keeping hold of her hand. They moved well together, as if they were naturally in tune with one another.

The children stopped dancing and made a circle around them, clapping their hands in time to the music.

Adam put his hand around Christina's waist and swung her around. Around and around they went as Karen began an even more lively tune. Christina felt light and balanced, as if her feet had sprouted wings.

The music grew faster. Adam swung her more quickly in time with it. They were moving so fast that her surroundings became a blur.

Suddenly, her foot hit a slick patch on the grass. Christina lost her balance, tumbling into Adam and knocking him off his feet. Together they fell onto the soft grass.

Karen stopped playing. "Are you all right?" she asked.

Adam burst out laughing. Christina laughed, too. All the children joined in. "Fine," Christina told Karen. "Just fine!"

Karen smiled and nodded. "Good," she said, reaching out to help Christina to her feet. "That was some dancing. You're great."

"Thanks," Christina replied, still a bit breathless. "It was really fun."

Christina realized that for the first time in a long while, she was smiling—smiling so hard her face hurt.

15

The next morning, Saturday, Christina woke up in a great mood. She'd dreamt about Ned, Edwina, and Norma, the angels. In her dream, she was at the bridge talking to them. She couldn't remember what they'd been saying, but she knew she'd felt happy to be with them. She'd felt so safe and loved.

She got out of bed and thought about the day before.

After her dance with Adam, the two of them had said good-bye and hurried through the woods together. She'd reached the back of the stable just as the last rays of sun had disappeared from the sky. "Will you be able to find your way back in the dark?" Christina had asked him.

"No problem," he'd said confidently. "I know every inch of these woods."

"I had a great time," she'd told him.

"Me, too," he'd said and then had turned and disappeared from view, seeming to melt into the darkening woods.

Christina sat forward in bed and thought about Adam. Was she falling in love with him? She was so happy when she was with him. He made her feel so good about herself. Was that what love *really* felt like?

"Christina!" her mother called from the hallway. She knocked and then poked her head into the room. "Remember you're helping me with that trail ride today."

Christina had forgotten all about it. She swung her long legs over the side of the bed. "I'll be right there."

"Thanks," her mother said, moving away from the door.

"Mom," Christina said. "I'm sorry about yesterday—that I was so crabby and all."

Alice nodded thoughtfully. "That's all right. Are you feeling better?"

"Sort of, yeah," Christina admitted.

"Good," her mother said with a smile. "Now, hurry."

Christina dressed quickly. When she reached the kitchen her mother was pouring herself a bowlful of granola. "Have some," she urged Christina.

It looked appealing to Christina. She loved the nutty taste of granola. Especially the health-food store brand her mom bought.

"No, thanks," she decided. Despite her good mood, she wasn't ready to jump into eating a bowl of granola. Anything that tasted that good *had* to be fattening.

Adam and Karen were nice, she reflected, but maybe

they had a different idea of what looked good. Now that she was home, she still felt she needed to lose a few more pounds.

"Honey, you have got to eat!" Alice said warningly.

Christina snapped off a branch of green grapes from the fruit bowl on the counter and popped two into her mouth. They were wonderfully sweet, but they made Christina's stomach grumble for more food. More *real* food.

Hurrying back to her room, Christina grabbed the package of Fat Away from her top drawer. She popped two in her mouth.

Christina waited a moment for the growling in her stomach to stop. It did. Christina heaved a sigh of relief.

The Fat Away *did* work. Maybe. Christina certainly felt less like eating after taking them. They made her feel slightly queasy, enough so the idea of eating was unappealing. Christina hated the feeling. But she didn't want to eat, either.

"A handful of grapes is not breakfast," her mother said when she returned to the kitchen. She pointed down to the open newspaper in front of her. "Your horoscope says you need to make a big change," she said.

"It does?" said Christina. "That probably means I need to lose weight."

"I doubt it," Alice disagreed. "Christina, do you ever look in the mirror? You are *not* fat. At all."

"What does my horoscope say, exactly?" Christina asked, hoping to deflect her mother.

"Aquarius. Change is in the air. The dark clouds are clearing, and a light will soon be shed on your current situation," Alice read.

"Hmmmm," Christina pondered. "It sounds interesting. I have no idea what it could possibly mean."

"It means you should eat something," her mother said firmly.

With an exasperated moan, Christina snapped off another branch of grapes and began eating. "How's that?"

"Better than nothing, I guess," her mother said with grim resignation.

They walked together down to the stable. Riders were already gathered outside waiting for them. Seeing Molly among the waiting riders—alone, this time—Christina scowled darkly.

"I have this gift certificate," Molly told Alice, waving a pink slip in the air. "Mr. Kingsley gave it to us to make up for that disaster the last time."

Alice took the slip and looked at it. "Are you sure you want to ride again?" she asked skeptically.

"I can ride," Molly said haughtily. "Just don't give me the worst horse in the stable this time, and I'll be perfectly fine."

Christina rolled her eyes. What a brat she was!

"We'll give you a very nice horse," Alice said patiently.

Molly darted a glance at Christina but didn't bother to acknowledge her. That was fine by Christina. She didn't want anything to do with Molly, either.

"We'll go out in ten minutes," Alice told the group as she checked her watch. "At exactly nine o'clock."

In the stable, Christina helped her mother saddle the horses. "I'll take Bridey," she said.

"All right," Alice agreed. "We'll give your friend Daisy."

"She is *not* my friend," Christina said emphatically.

"Isn't she in your class at school?" Alice asked.

"That doesn't make us friends," Christina assured her mother.

By nine o'clock all eight riders were mounted and ready to set out on the trail.

With an arrogant toss of her long blonde hair Molly sat impatiently atop Daisy. Christina admired her delicate, fragile appearance. No wonder Matt liked her. Molly seemed almost fairylike as she sat there with the morning sun bouncing off her flowing hair.

Molly seemed a little agitated to Christina, almost as if she was anxious to meet someone or go somewhere. Christina decided she might simply be nervous about getting onto a horse again after what happened the last time.

Molly eyed Bridey with disdain. "It's your funeral," she muttered to Christina.

"I'm not worried," Christina replied tersely.

"Let's head out!" Alice gave the command, and the horses started moving. Molly was one of the last riders out. Christina and Bridey followed right behind, bringing up the rear.

Alice led them into the quiet, still dewy woods. They rode at a steady gait. The even-paced clip-clop of the horses created a lulling sound punctuated only by the occasional snapping of a branch or the distant call of a bird.

Christina disappeared into her own thoughts as she recalled her visit with Karen and the kids the day before. What an ideal life they had. Whatever they lost out on by living way out there on their own, or the children lost by not being in school, Christina was now convinced the family more than made up for it in the rich life—so close to nature, so close to one another—they led.

As she thought about them, she understood that the thing that impressed her most was how they all seemed so at ease with who they were. She'd never met people so completely comfortable with themselves. She'd never met people who seemed so happy.

The group came to a part of the trail where the pines stood very close together. It was a cool, shadowy spot. Soft pine boughs swept Christina's cheek as they rode through.

Molly turned abruptly to Christina. "My one riding boot is killing me," she said. "I'm going to stop and fix it."

"You're not supposed to leave the group," Christina said stiffly.

"Tough," Molly told her. "I'm getting a blister. All I have to do is fix my sock, and then it won't rub."

"Well, do it quickly," Christina said coldly.

Molly steered Daisy just off the path to the far side of a thick pine. Christina slowed Bridey but continued on. She wasn't about to wait around for Molly like some sort of lowly servant.

She turned and watched Molly as she dismounted. Molly glanced up and, for a moment, their eyes met. Then Molly turned her attention to pulling off her soft, brown leather riding boots.

That girl really thinks she's hot stuff, Christina thought irritably. *She'd probably like the whole line to stop just so she can fix her million-dollar boots.*

But as Christina slowly rode on with Bridey, she became aware of an uneasy nagging tugging at the corner of her brain.

What was it?

Was it one of her hunches, one of the intuitions she often had?

A picture popped into Christina's head. It was of Molly's face, of the look on her face when their eyes had met. Molly's eyes were troubled and furtive, as if she were about to do something she shouldn't.

Christina looked back sharply over her shoulder and gasped.

Molly had disappeared.

16

Impulsively, without alerting the group, Christina snapped Bridey's reins and cantered back to the spot where she'd last seen Molly. She sat tall in the saddle, checking in every direction.

Then she spotted her, off a number of yards to the right, camouflaged by the trees.

What does that spoiled brat think she's doing? Christina wondered, filled with outrage.

"Come on, Bridey," Christina said, leaning forward in the saddle. "She's not running off with Daisy. I'm not getting into trouble because of her."

Pressing her knees hard into Bridey's sides, Christina urged the horse on as fast as she could go through the narrowly spaced trees.

It didn't take long for Christina to close the space between Molly and herself.

Molly turned and saw Christina approaching. She kicked Daisy hard and began to gallop through the woods.

Christina did the same. *You're not getting away from me,* she thought with fierce determination.

Sweat beaded Christina's forehead as she squeezed Bridey ever more tightly, letting out the reins and urging her to go faster. The space between Molly and herself was definitely closing, but Molly continued to stay ahead.

"Molly!" Christina shouted. "Molly, stop!"

But Molly kept going, kicking up a spray of dirt and fallen pine needles behind her.

Christina followed her up a hill. She could hear the noise of the creek on the other side. She knew they must be close to the Angels Crossing Bridge.

From the top of the hill, Christina could see Molly at the entrance to the bridge below. She was about to gallop across when Daisy abruptly came to a halt.

"*Go!*" Molly screamed at the horse. "Go, you stupid animal!"

Daisy whinnied stubbornly and pawed the ground with her foreleg.

Clicking to Bridey, Christina rode down the hill.

Molly looked up and scowled at her. She jerked the reins hard, but still Daisy wouldn't go forward. "Go, you stupid horse!" Molly screamed. "Go!"

"What's the big idea?" Christina demanded angrily when she was close to Molly. "*What* do you think you're doing?"

Molly's face flushed with anger and irritation. Wispy strands of hair were plastered to her sweaty forehead and high, sharp cheekbones. Her eyes seemed larger than usual, and there was a desperate, trapped look in them.

Panting and out of breath, she faced Christina.

For a moment, neither girl spoke.

There was something in Molly's expression that stopped Christina from raging at her.

What was it?

She wasn't sure.

"What's going on, Molly?" she asked. "You can tell me."

"Nothing!" Molly swung her leg over Daisy's saddle as she began to dismount. "None of your business!"

"It *is* my business," Christina insisted firmly. "You're running off with one of the ranch's horses. That's my business."

The scared, pathetic expression melted from Molly's face. Replacing it was the hard, arrogant look Christina was used to seeing there. "Just get out of my face, loser!" Molly snapped, brushing past Daisy and heading toward the bridge.

"Where are you going!" Christina asked angrily. "Molly, stop it!"

"Buzz off!" Molly called back to her.

Dismounting quickly, Christina ran after her. As long as Molly was riding with the group, she was responsible for her. She couldn't let her just stomp off into the woods.

Just inside the bridge, Christina caught up and grabbed Molly's arm. "What's with you?" she shouted angrily. "Are you crazy?"

"What do you care?" Molly replied, spitting out the words. She wrenched her arm free of Christina's grasp. "Just let me go!"

"Where are you going?" Christina cried.

Molly's pale face suddenly twisted into a pained expression. "Away!" she blurted as tears poured down her face. "They're not locking *me* up in some hospital. I don't care what you say! I'm not crazy! I'm not going!"

"Hospital? Crazy?" Christina gasped. "What are you talking about?"

Leaning against the bridge's railing, Molly roughly brushed away her tears. "The stupid doctor keeps telling my parents I'm too thin. He says if I don't stop losing weight, I'm going to have to go to the hospital."

Christina took a hard look at Molly. Beneath her expensive silk T-shirt, Christina could actually see her ribs. Now that she looked close, now that she really paid attention, Christina could see that Molly's collarbone jutted forward much more prominently than was normal. Now, too, she realized why Molly's eyes seemed so large and her cheekbones so sharp. It was because her face was so extremely, incredibly thin.

"The hospital?" Christina repeated. "Why to the hospital?"

Molly shook her head miserably. "They have some

program there for people with eating disorders. That's what they say I have."

"If you don't want to go, then just eat some more. Even if you gained weight, you'd still be thin," Christina offered.

Molly turned from Christina and gazed out over the creek. "I can't," she said passionately. "When I look into the mirror, all I see is this fat slob!" she wailed.

"But you're not . . . you're . . . not, that's . . ." Christina stammered, shocked by Molly's words.

"Crazy?" Molly finished.

"Yeah. I mean I was going to say that, but . . . but, you're not crazy. You're not. So how can you possibly think you're fat?"

"I do, I just do," Molly said desperately.

"Is it because of Matt?" Christina asked quietly. "Does he want you to be thinner?"

A bitter laugh came from Molly. "No," she answered. "He always told me I was too thin. But who cares about him, anyway? We broke up last week."

"You did?" Christina asked, bewildered. This was good news, but Molly's misery made it hard for Christina to feel happy.

Molly nodded. "All we did was fight about my eating. He said he couldn't take it anymore. We didn't have that much in common, anyway."

"If you ran away, where would you go?" Christina asked.

Molly shrugged. "I don't know. Someplace where I don't have to be perfect all the time."

"Who says you have to be perfect here?" Christina asked, puzzled.

"My parents," Molly said sadly. "And do you want to know the really sick part? *I* say I have to be perfect, too. I've been listening to them for so long, it's as if their voices are inside my head now. No matter what I do, I feel like it isn't good enough. I'm not smart enough, popular enough, pretty enough, thin enough."

"But, Molly, you must know that's not true," Christina told her earnestly.

"It is," Molly contradicted her flatly.

"If you feel that way, then there's really no place you can run to, is there?" Christina said softly.

"Maybe I'll find a place."

"Listen, Molly, why don't you come back with me? I have to bring Daisy back, but you come, too. Okay?"

Molly shook her head violently. "No. No way. I'm not going to let them take me away and force me to eat. I'd rather die."

"You can't just run off into these woods. I get lost out here sometimes, and I've been around these woods most of my life. If you get really lost, you could die out here."

Molly muttered something that Christina couldn't hear. "What did you say?" she asked.

Whirling around suddenly, Molly shouted at Christina. "I *said* that *might* not be such a bad thing!" She ran toward the center of the bridge.

"Molly! Come back!" Christina cried, running after her. *What was Molly doing?* she wondered.

As she ran, Christina suddenly saw a blindingly bright white spot floating at the edge of the bridge. Its brightness was so intense she had to turn away. She shut her eyes tightly. Red spots floated behind the blackness of her lids as though she'd just been staring at the white-hot center of the sun.

Had Molly seen it, too?

Christina opened her eyes in time to see the spot suddenly burst open, expanding until it seemed to fill the bridge.

Molly was caught in its brilliant illumination and thrown off her feet. She came flying back toward Christina.

Shielding herself with her arms, Christina grunted heavily as Molly slammed into her.

Together, the two girls tumbled backward.

17

Christina struggled to breathe. Molly had hit her with such force she'd had the wind knocked out of her.

The blinding light was no longer on the bridge.

Everything was back to normal.

But where was Molly?

Turning, she saw Molly sitting on the ground behind her, clutching her head.

Karen and Adam were bending over her.

Adam met Christina's eyes. "Are you all right?"

Slowly opening her mouth, Christina croaked out the words in short, gasping breaths. "Yes, I think so."

Adam moved to her side and placed his hand gently between her shoulder blades. "Take just small breaths for now," he advised. "Karen and I were near the bridge. We saw you two fall backward, so we came to see if you were all right."

Karen looked over to Christina. "What happened to you girls?" she asked in alarm.

Christina shook her head and shrugged in bewilderment. She looked at Molly. She'd been closer to the light. Maybe she knew.

But Molly seemed barely aware of them. With wide eyes, she stared blankly into space.

"I think she's in shock," Karen said. "The light. I saw light coming from the bridge. What was it?"

"I don't know," Christina managed to reply as the air returned to her lungs.

"At least you're both all right," Adam said.

"I'm not sure Molly *is* all right," Christina answered. "Look at her."

"No, she doesn't seem to be with it," Karen agreed, studying Molly's vacant face. "We'd better get her some help. You girls rode those horses here?"

And that was another weird thing, Christina thought. Normally something as strange as what had just happened would have really spooked the horses—especially Bridey, who was so skittish to begin with. Yet there they stood, calmly nibbling the grass and looking as content and quiet as cows.

Still, she decided to say nothing about that. Nodding to Karen, Christina stood. "I can either go for help or try to get her into the saddle and let Daisy carry her back. I wonder if she's well enough to ride back."

"Let's try to get her up," Karen suggested. She turned to Molly. "Come on, hon. Can you get up?"

Molly just sat, holding her head and staring.

"Molly," Christina coaxed gently. "Molly."

The girl looked up at her, but the blank, stunned expression stayed on her face.

"She needs looking after. Why don't we carry her?" Karen said. "Take her legs." She lifted Molly under her arms. Christina took her legs. Molly didn't protest. She didn't seem to realize she was being moved.

Molly felt feather-light. Her lightness shocked Christina. She felt as if she was lifting a child.

"My little Melody weighs more than this girl," Karen commented.

Daisy and Bridey waited patiently at the entrance to the bridge. Together, Christina and Karen boosted Molly into the saddle. Adam stood on the other side of Daisy and reached up to make sure she didn't fall all the way over.

To Christina's surprise, Molly sat upright. She'd expected her to slump forward or over somehow. Still, Molly didn't take the reins. Christina wondered if she even knew she was on a horse.

Christina looked up at Molly and shook her head. "She's not going to make it on horseback," she said. "She'll fall."

"I'd get up there with her, but horses and me don't mix," Karen said. "I spent six months in a leg cast once, thanks to a horse."

"I'll get up," Adam offered. With amazing grace he leaped into the saddle behind Molly. Reaching around her, he took hold of the reins.

"Maybe we should lay her across the saddle," Karen suggested.

"I think she'll be all right," Christina said.

"I hope so," Karen said with an anxious glance up at Molly.

Christina climbed atop Bridey and nodded. "You didn't see what caused that light?" she asked Karen and Adam.

"No," Karen said. "It was the strangest thing. I was in the woods, and suddenly there was this flash. Maybe it was some sort of weird dry summer lightning."

"It was more like a ball of light," Christina said speculatively, trying to see it all over again. "It started as a ball but turned more into an oval shape at the end."

"Strange," Karen murmured.

"We'd better go," Christina said. She clicked softly to Bridey and began moving.

"Oh, Christina," Karen called after her as if a thought had suddenly come to her. "Will you be at the Miller's Creek Summer Fest?"

Miller's Creek was a town near Pine Ridge. Every summer there was a fair there, in the large town park. "Mom and I usually go," Christina answered. "Why?"

"I'll be selling my honey and my carvings there," Karen said. "Look for me."

"I will," Christina agreed with a wave.

They trotted through the woods side by side. "Are you feeling all right?" Adam asked.

"My back hurts where I hit when I fell, but I think I'm

okay," she replied. "What do you think that could have been? Do you think it was lightning?"

Adam shrugged. "Hard to say," was all he said.

They rode for awhile in silence before Adam spoke. "Are you feeling any better about your dancing and all?" he wanted to know.

"I don't know," Christina admitted. "Being asked to leave class really was a disappointment. It made me feel so . . . so . . . dumb. You know, like a real klutz."

"You're not a klutz," Adam said. "The way you danced the other day proved that."

"Thanks," Christina said. His words really meant a lot to her. He was one of the nicest, most sincere people she'd ever met. She couldn't imagine him lying. "Do you really mean that?" she asked.

"Sure. Of course, I do. You were flying," he said with his gorgeous, warm smile.

They had ridden a few minutes longer when Christina heard a worried voice calling in the distance. "Christina! Molly!"

It was her mother.

"Over here!" she shouted back. "We're here!"

With Alice in the lead, the group of riders approached through the trees. Christina raised her arm in a broad wave. "Here we are!"

As her mother neared, her face was angry. But when she caught sight of Molly her scowl melted into a look of concern. "What's wrong? What happened?" she asked Christina. "Why did you girls ride off like that?"

Christina wasn't sure how to reply. She decided that the important thing now was to get Molly to a doctor, not to get entangled in long explanations of strange lights.

"She lost control of the horse again, and I went after her," Christina lied. "She fell and hit her head. I think she's in shock or something." That part, at least, was true.

Christina remembered she hadn't introduced Adam. "Oh, Mom, this is my friend," she said, turning toward Adam. "His name is—"

She glanced all around quickly.

How could it be?

Adam was gone. Vanished into thin air.

18

"It's really nice of you to want to visit," Katie commented the next day as they entered Saint Anne's Hospital. "It's not like Molly's ever been particularly nice to you. I don't get it."

"I just want to see how she is," Christina explained, shifting the bouquet of flowers she'd brought from one hand to the other. "It's like you said about the girls at your old school. Some of them aren't as bad as they seem. Molly and I talked a little before the . . . uh, accident. She's dealing with a lot of things we didn't know about."

"A lot of people have problems. It doesn't mean you can get away with being obnoxious," Katie remarked.

Christina shrugged. "This will only take a few minutes. Then we can go over to the Miller's Creek fair from here. We can't stay long, anyway," Christina went on. "The trail ride Ashley took out should be ending about now. She said she'd meet us at the front gate and it won't take her long to get there."

"All right," Katie agreed. "I'll wait out here for you."

"Come on in," Christina urged her.

"She doesn't want to see me."

Christina took hold of Katie's arm and gently drew her toward the hospital room. "Come on."

"Oh, all right," Katie said grudgingly. "But let's make it quick. I don't want to leave Ashley standing around waiting forever."

Christina knocked on the open door and stepped inside. Molly's bed was raised to the sitting position. A pole at her side supported a liquid-filled bag with a tube that was attached to the bend in Molly's bony arm.

Molly sat with pillows plumped around her, writing on a pad propped on her bent legs. The half-opened blinds let in bands of sunshine that striped Molly's pale, thin form. In her hospital gown she looked thinner and more fragile than ever.

"Hi, Molly," Christina said softly.

The girl turned, and a small, soft smile formed on her face.

Christina instantly recalled Molly's old, tight smile. This wasn't it. This wasn't the same smile at all. In fact, her entire face appeared transformed. Molly's gaunt, perfect features were the same, and yet her expression was entirely different. It was softer, more pleasant, and it gave her such a different look that Christina wouldn't have been surprised if someone told her this wasn't Molly at all, but a cousin or sister.

Glancing at Katie, Christina saw that she, too, had registered the change in Molly's appearance. Her brows were knit in confusion.

"How are you feeling?" Christina asked, laying the flowers on the little table beside the bed.

"All right," she replied in a quiet voice. "Good, really. Very good."

"That thing in your arm doesn't look too comfortable," Katie said in a jolly, uneasy voice.

"It's not bad," said Molly. "You forget it's even there after awhile. It's got sugar and vitamins and all that stuff in it, to keep me strong."

"That's good, I guess," Katie said.

Christina was glad to see that Molly no longer seemed to be in shock. "Did they tell you what was the matter with you?" she asked.

"The doctor here said I'm malnourished. That's why they hooked up this IV thing here," Molly explained.

"But the light," Christina questioned. "Were you in shock or something? Did it do anything to you?"

"It made me happy."

"Huh?" Christina said, bewildered.

Molly sat forward in bed. "You're going to think I'm crazy," she said, her voice almost a whisper. "But there was someone inside the light." She stopped to check their reactions, then continued. "It was a woman, a very tall woman, like a giant. But she was so gentle. She didn't seem to move her mouth, but I could hear her in my head."

"What was she saying?" Katie asked, moving closer to the bed.

Molly's eyes darted to the ceiling and then to the window, as if she were deciding whether or not she should answer, if she could trust them. "She said she loved me."

"She loved you," Christina echoed quietly.

Molly nodded. "She said other things to me, too, but I can't remember the exact words. But, you know, it's like when you have a dream. You can't remember the exact words, but you remember the feelings."

"And you felt happy?" Christina asked.

"So happy," said Molly. "But . . . but, what do you think it was? I'm not crazy. I know you saw it, too, Christina."

"I *did* see it," Christina admitted. "Although all I saw was the light. I didn't see the person . . . or being . . . or whatever it was, inside."

Katie and Christina looked at one another searchingly. *Did Molly see an angel?* Christina wondered. She knew Katie was wondering the same thing.

"She had wings," Molly said softly. "She looked like an angel. A huge, gorgeous angel."

"Ohmygosh," Katie said in a low rush.

"Oh, I know it sounds crazy," said Molly, "but—"

"It's *not* crazy," Christina cut her off. "You were on the Angels Crossing Bridge. We've met angels there, too."

"You have?" Molly gasped. "Then, I'm not . . . crazy."

"No, you're not," Katie told her. "Either that, or we're crazy, too."

Relief flooded Molly's face. "I didn't want to tell my parents or the doctors about it, because I figured they'd think I was delirious with malnutrition or out of my head completely."

"We know how you feel," Christina assured her.

Molly glanced at the intravenous bag by her side. "This may sound weird, but I'm feeling so good about things that I'm actually glad they hooked me up to this. I want to get better, to get on with things. I can't wait to get out of here and start doing things differently."

"What would you do differently?" Katie asked.

Molly's face grew thoughtful. "I want to start being myself, not the person I think everyone will like." She nodded down at the pad on her lap. "I started writing my parents a letter, trying to tell them that. I hope they'll understand."

"I hope so, too," Christina responded. "I bet they will."

Just then Matt walked into the room. Christina felt her heartbeat quicken at the sight of him. "Hi," he said to Katie and Christina. "Hi, Molly."

Molly's face lit up.

Christina looked from Molly to Matt. It was clear that despite the fact that they'd split up, their relationship wasn't over. "I guess we should be going," she said tactfully. "Bye, Molly."

"Bye," she said. "Thanks for coming. And for . . . you know, listening. I haven't been very nice to you, Christina."

"I know," Christina teased with a smile. "Forget it." She was about to turn away when she remembered something. "Molly, did you know Matt believes in angels?"

Matt looked at Christina, puzzled. "Yeah, I do," he murmured.

Molly looked at Matt happily. "You do? I'm really glad to hear that."

"You are?" Matt asked, now looking totally bewildered. "Why?"

"Tell him," Christina urged Molly. "I'm pretty sure he'll understand."

When Katie and Christina were almost to the door, Christina thought of one last thing and turned back. "Molly, do you remember the guy who rode on the horse with you?"

Molly looked at her blankly. "No."

"Do you remember the ride back at all?" Christina asked.

"Not really," Molly admitted. "I sort of came to on the way to the hospital. Why?"

"Never mind," Christina said. "Feel better!"

Outside the hall, Katie turned to Christina. "You're still wondering about Adam, aren't you?"

"Of course I am," Christina said. "How could he have just vanished like that?"

"What if he slipped off the horse when you weren't looking and ran back into the woods," Katie suggested.

"Why would he do that?"

Katie's mouth twisted as she thought about this. "He could be shy. Maybe he freaked when he saw your mother and the other riders approaching."

"That could be," Christina considered. "He does live a pretty quiet life there in the woods. He might not be comfortable around a lot of people."

"That's probably it," Katie said.

"I guess," Christina said uncertainly. His disappearance still seemed very strange to her. "I wonder if he'll be at the fair. Karen said she'll have a stall there. I can't wait for you to meet her."

Katie hesitated a moment. "I just want to tell you I think it was really nice what you said to Molly about Matt believing in angels. She probably didn't even know that about him."

Christina glanced back into Molly's hospital room. Matt was sitting on the bed. He and Molly were hugging.

"Well, she knows it now. Come on. Let's go," Christina said. She felt oddly light, and happier than she'd felt in what seemed like ages.

19

Christina felt her spirits rise as the Ferris wheel came into view. Once a year the Miller's Creek fair took over the large gently rolling hills of the Miller's Creek Town Park.

The hospital was within walking distance of the fair, so Katie and Christina were able to walk right past the cars lined up out into the road, waiting to pay their parking fee.

When they reached the ticket booth at the front of the fairgrounds, Ashley was waiting. "Hi!" she greeted them with a wave. "Your mom, Christina, and mine already went in. I said I'd wait for you here. How's Molly?"

"She's a totally different person," Katie told her excitedly. "That light she and Christina saw on the bridge—it was an angel. It spoke to her and told her to stop acting like such a little witch."

Christina pushed Katie. "That's *not* what she told her. How can you joke about it like that?"

"Tell me!" Ashley prodded. "What *did* she say?"

Christina told Ashley exactly what Molly had said.

"That's awesome," Ashley commented. "And guess what happened to me this afternoon while I was on the trail with a group of riders?"

"What?" Katie asked.

"Well, I saw three people walking through the woods—a blonde woman, a black-haired woman, and a man with longish brown hair."

"Edwina, Norma, and Ned!" Christina cried excitedly. "Did you talk to them?"

"Well, at first I thought they were just a group of bird watchers. They were dressed in these baggy clothes, and they had binoculars. One of them let out the most beautiful bird call, and a bird actually answered."

"So how did you know it was them?" Katie asked.

"Ned turned and waved to me," Ashley replied. "I could see his face. It was him, all right. I looked over to the riders. I was checking to see if I could leave for a moment and go speak to Ned, Norma, and Edwina. When I looked back, they were gone."

"I wonder why they picked now to appear," Christina mused.

"I don't know," Ashley replied.

They stood silently a moment, thinking about this. Then they turned and went into the fair.

As soon as they entered the fair grounds, the unique,

unmistakable smells of the fair washed over Christina. She was instantly reminded of past fairs—of the smells of sugary cotton candy, sizzling sausage, and powdery funnel cakes; of grease from the machinery that moved the big rides, such as the roller coaster and the Whip-It; and of the musky odor of hay and livestock that wafted up from the 4-H tents.

The girls started on the roller coaster and then lined up for the Whip-It. They were determined to go on every ride.

When they reached the top of the Ferris wheel, overlooking the fair, the wheel stopped to let on more riders. The first pink and gold of the approaching sunset swept across the sky. A breeze tossed the tops of the trees surrounding the grounds. Christina's eyes took in the entire grounds, looking for Adam or for Karen's stall. She didn't see either.

"When you're up here, the world seems very far away, doesn't it," Ashley murmured wistfully. "Little things don't seem so important up here."

"Yeah, you really get the *big* picture," Katie joked with an expansive sweep of her arms, rocking the Ferris wheel car slightly.

Christina wondered if this was how it felt to be an angel, hovering above everything.

The wheel began turning again. It went around several times more before the ride ended.

The girls got off the Ferris wheel and roamed through the fairgrounds. They petted the cows and sheep. Katie won a small stuffed dinosaur by tossing rubber frogs onto floating plastic lilypads in a steel pond.

By the time they reached the crafts tent, the sunset was fully exploded, washing everything in golden light. "There's Karen's stall," Christina cried, pointing down the long, narrow tent.

Christina led the way as they hurried over to Karen. "Hi," Karen greeted them warmly. She stood in front of a table on which were set out detailed, graceful carvings.

"This is beautiful," Ashley said, gently lifting a foot-high carved figure of a winged angel carrying two babies.

"Thank you," Karen said. "It's one of my favorites."

The girls looked over all the figures, admiring their beauty and the skill they knew it had taken to carve them. Karen gave them samples of the honey she had harvested from the bees she kept. She was selling it at a table next to her carvings.

"I'm getting hungry," Katie said.

"Me, too," Ashley agreed. "I'll go to the food area and bring back anything anyone would like."

Karen gave Ashley money to bring back a sausage sandwich. "I guess you don't want anything, do you?" Ashley asked Christina. "I mean, I know you're dieting."

Shaking her head in disagreement, Christina took a five-dollar bill from her pocket. "Would you get me a piece of that fried funnel cake with the powdered sugar on it? Lots of powdered sugar?"

Ashley's eyes went wide. "Really?"

"I love that funnel cake, and you can only get it here once a year, at the fair," Christina said. "I can't pass it up."

"*All right*," Katie cheered. "The girl has come to her senses!"

Katie and Ashley went off to bring back food. Christina stood beside Karen's stall and watched while she sold a jar of honey to a passerby.

"Why do you carve angels?" Christina asked, examining a thoughtful, seated angel carved in a deep cherry-brown wood.

"I've always loved the idea of angels, and I believe they're real. And when we moved to our place in the woods many years ago, I began dreaming of angels. I still dream about them all the time."

Christina nodded.

Karen leaned closer to Christina and dropped her voice. "I'll tell you something strange. Ever since my husband died, I've had the strongest feeling that someone—an angel, perhaps—is very close by us all the time, looking out for the kids and me."

"I saw an angel one day," Christina confided. "It led me to your house."

Karen's dark eyes bored into Christina's as though she were trying to see into Christina's heart, trying to tell if she was serious.

"I wouldn't lie," Christina assured her. "I've seen angels there in the woods. That light on the bridge the other day was an angel. She was there to help Molly, the girl we carried."

A mist of tears swept across Karen's eyes. She placed her hand over her heart. "I believe you," she said. "I've never seen an angel, but the most amazing things have happened."

"Like what?" Christina asked.

Karen thought a moment. "Like our food. I shop once a week, but it's never enough. Someone else leaves me food. Sometimes I'll get a basketful of berries. Once I found a bucket of milk. It was still warm, as if someone had just milked a cow and then delivered it to my doorstep. But the nearest dairy farm is too far for someone to milk a cow and deliver it, still warm. You've had some of the mysterious food yourself. Those wild turkeys. Three of them were lying at my doorstep that morning."

"I thought Adam hunted those for you," Christina said.

Karen blinked hard. "Adam?"

"Your nephew, or whoever he is."

Shaking her head, Karen's expression remained blank. "I don't know anyone named Adam."

"You know—Adam," Christina insisted passionately.

"I heard you say something about someone named Adam. What was it? You said Adam told you something or other. I just assumed Adam was a friend of yours."

Christina's mind reeled. What was Karen talking about? Of course Karen knew him. "Adam. You were on the bridge with him the other day."

"No, I was alone," Karen said.

This was crazy! What was she saying? "I danced with Adam at your house! You saw him!"

"You were dancing by yourself, Christina," Karen said gently.

Christina's breath started coming more heavily as her thoughts raced. It was true—she couldn't remember ever seeing Karen speak directly to Adam. And Mariah and Melody hadn't known who he was, either.

A couple stopped to look at Karen's carvings. While Karen's attention was diverted, Christina wandered off, down toward the far end of the tent.

Her mind spun. Adam was invisible. He wasn't there. She was the only one who saw him. Was he a ghost? Some kind of spirit? Why was she the only one who could see him?

She stood at the open end of the tent. The sun had nearly set. In front of her was a large, low wooden platform, strung with colored lantern lights. As she watched, the lanterns suddenly snapped on, throwing colored light onto the platform.

A sound speaker mounted on a pole beside the platform crackled to life. "Ladies and gentlemen. The Clyde Parkins bluegrass country band will be playing next to the crafts tent. Anyone wishing to come join them is welcome to dance along."

Four elderly men in jeans, patchwork shirts, and straw hats carried fiddles up and settled themselves on chairs in the corner of the makeshift stage. Slowly, people started moving toward the platform.

Christina hung on the center pole of the crafts tent, remembering dancing with Adam while Karen played. He'd seemed so real. She'd felt the warmth of his strong hand.

The musicians began playing a lively song. Several couples moved out onto the platform.

Christina watched them for a moment. Suddenly she had the sensation of being stared at. She looked over toward the corner of the platform.

There stood Adam, in jeans and a T-shirt.

20

He smiled and held out his hand to her.

Christina froze.

But his smile was so warm. She was so comfortable with him.

"Come on, I don't bite," he said, his arm still outstretched, his hand open. Christina gazed into his clear blue eyes and stepped forward.

He met her at the top of the platform's wooden stairs.

She had to talk to him. There was so much to ask him.

But he put his hand around her waist and swung her out onto the platform. Around and around they went in perfect step with the music, in perfect step with one another.

As she spun, Christina's spirits soared. She felt the same elation she'd felt that day at Karen's.

She suddenly realized things she hadn't understood until that moment. She'd felt accepted and comfortable with Adam. She'd felt beautiful.

And she'd learned she could dance. She wasn't a clumsy moose!

The music got faster. She and Adam picked up their pace.

"Eeeeee-yaaaa-hhaaaaa!" whooped one of the musicians.

Christina glanced at him for no more than a second. When she looked back toward Adam, he was bathed in a golden light.

And Adam had wings!

Huge wings with gleaming, iridescent white feathers. He still wore his jeans and T-shirt, but now his incredible wings fanned out behind him.

Speechless, Christina let herself be spun across the platform.

From the corner of her eye, she saw Katie and Ashley watching her, their arms loaded with bags and plates of food. Katie's jaw hung in awe, while Ashley stared, wide-eyed.

Could they see Adam's wings? Could they see Adam?

Christina looked around. No one else was paying any attention to them. But Katie and Ashley must be able to see what was going on. She could tell from their faces.

As Christina looked around, she caught sight of three people dancing in a triangle. They looked like real hill people. The man wore baggy overalls. The women wore gingham dresses with puffed sleeves. But something about them was very familiar.

They seemed to be having the most wonderful time. Their arms hooked together, then flew apart as they swung one another around in a square-dance-style loop.

Then the man turned and smiled at her.

Right away, Christina knew. It was Ned. Ned, Edwina, and Norma!

Adam danced Christina over near their circle. They joined them, linking arms and dancing in a circle.

In a blink Ned, Edwina, and Norma changed from simple country folk to shimmering angels—but they kept dancing.

Christina's heart soared.

She didn't care if it looked as if she were out of her mind, dancing up there all alone. She didn't care if everyone thought she was a crazy person.

She knew who she was and what she was doing. And that was all that mattered.

She was fine the way she was.

She was dancing with angels!

FOREVER ANGELS

KATIE'S ANGEL

by Suzanne Weyn

Katie thought she was all alone in the world . . .

When her parents died, Katie's world turned upside down. Forced to move in with uncaring relatives, she's never felt more alone. Katie can't stop missing her parents, and it seems she's always getting into trouble for one reason or another. Finally she can't take it any longer and decides to run away. And that's when Katie discovers that she's not as alone as she thinks she is. There's someone special looking out for her—someone she never would have guessed—who can help Katie find the happiness she's been missing.

0-8167-3614-6
$3.25 U.S. / $4.50 Can.

Available wherever you buy books.

FOREVER ANGELS

ASHLEY'S LOST ANGEL

by Suzanne Weyn

Ashley's searching for a miracle

Perfect Ashley's perfect life is suddenly falling apart. The boy she likes doesn't like her anymore, her grades are sinking, and her horse is sick. But that's nothing compared to her parents' problems. Their money troubles may force them to close their horse farm and give up the only home Ashley's ever known. Worst of all, they're even talking about getting a divorce. Ashley's desperate for an answer, something that can turn her life around. Is anyone listening?

A Special Preview

of

The Baby Angel

Katie stopped short, all her senses alert. A very strange sound had suddenly risen up around her. She wasn't sure what it was, but it was very, very close by.

Then Katie gasped as the realization hit her: *It's a baby. A baby crying alone in the woods.*

What was a baby doing in the woods? By itself?

Cocking her head attentively, Katie listened hard. The cries were so compelling, she couldn't ignore them.

She started up the hill, following the direction of the cries. At the top, the woods changed startlingly. Birch trees stood side by side, their white bark shining, their silvery autumn leaves shimmering in the breeze. Katie had never seen anything but pines in this woods before.

She walked through the trees, looking around as she went. The awful shrieking grew louder, telling Katie she was approaching the source.

As Katie neared a mossy boulder, she froze. Whatever was making the noise was behind the boulder.

Cautiously, Katie flattened herself against the cool rock and moved closer to the sound. Peering over the boulder, she cried out in surprise.

A red-faced baby in a pink one-piece stretchy suit lay sprawled at the base of the boulder, crying piteously.

Katie quickly checked around. Where were the parents? There was no sign of anyone.

"Poor baby," Katie cooed as she rushed to pick her up. The moment she lifted the child, the yowling subsided to pitiful breathy sobs.

Katie rocked gently and patted the baby's heaving back. "It's all right," she soothed. "It's all right."

Fat tears rolled down the baby's soft

cheeks. Her wet eyes gleamed and reminded Katie of a stone she'd seen in the nature store at the Pine Ridge Mall; hematite, a shiny black rock with flecks of shifting colors that changed as you rolled it in your hand.

She ran her hand across the dark, fuzzy wisps of hair atop the baby's warm head. "Don't cry. Your mom will be right back."

Wouldn't she?

* * *

The light was dying. Shadows of deep magenta, wavering dark purple and rich forest green slowly advanced, blanketing the once sun-dappled scenery.

Katie had waited with the baby for a long time. She wasn't sure how long because she didn't wear a watch. But she could tell from the light it was getting late.

A brisk gust of wind ruffled the trees and sent a shower of silver birch leaves fluttering to the ground. Katie shivered. Her jeans and T-shirt had been fine when she'd left home hours ago. Now it was getting cooler.

The baby in her arms hollered once in a

high, loud voice, calling to Katie for attention. Katie looked down and tickled her gently under her plump, soft chin. The baby chortled, revealing two small white bottom teeth.

Again, the baby shouted out, not unhappily, but as if she were trying to say something, to ask a question. “You don’t know me, do you?” Katie said softly. “It’s okay. I’m a friend. Don’t worry.”

The baby frowned, her smooth brow wrinkling, her expression still questioning. Katie felt like she should do something to communicate back. But what?

A lullaby might reassure her. Babies liked lullabies. “Hi, hi, my angel pie,” Katie crooned to the baby. Her mother used to sing that to her, to Katie, when *she* was small. It was the only lullaby she still remembered because even after she was no longer a baby, her mother often greeted her that way.

“Hi, hi, my angel pie.”

Katie paused, trying to recall the next verse. The baby looked up at her expectantly with her trusting, dark, hematite eyes.

The next verse was something about barefoot angels at the gates of heaven. Someone was making little shoes for them, Katie seemed to remember. She wasn't quite sure.

The baby gurgled to Katie in her soft, unintelligible baby talk.

Katie leaned closer to listen. "What are you saying, little baby-baby? Where's your mama, huh?"

Peering around, Katie looked for any clue she might have missed earlier when she first searched the area—something that would tell her where this baby's parents had gone or who they were.

Her earlier search had revealed only the ashes of a burned out campfire and a brown grocery bag containing a small plastic flashlight, another stretchy baby outfit, a pacifier and a small, faded rag doll.

Now, suddenly, she spotted something she'd overlooked before. A white cylinder lay among the silvery mat of fallen birch leaves on the ground.

Stooping with the baby nestled in the crook of her arm, Katie picked it up. It was a baby bottle, half full but carefully re-capped.

Katie unscrewed the cap and smelled the

liquid. It smelled okay. Wrinkling her nose and preparing for the worst, she cautiously sipped it. Not bad. It wasn't milk, though. Baby formula, probably.

The baby began to fuss, moving her head from side to side while making small cranking grumbles. "Okay, okay," Katie said gently. "Here you go." Katie held the bottle to the baby's lips and instantly she took hold, voraciously guzzling the formula.

Katie laughed softly, pleased that she'd made the baby happy. She moved to the boulder and slid to the ground with her back against the mossy rock. As the baby drank, Katie felt her small, impossibly soft hand wrap around Katie's thumb, her grip surprisingly strong.

"Aahh," Katie sighed happily. The baby was *so* sweet. A new feeling swept through her. She wasn't sure what it was. She felt this way a little when she handled her kitten, Nagle. But this feeling was much stronger, as if something in her heart had actually physically moved.

When the bottle was nearly empty, the baby's eyes grew heavy and her black-lashed lids drooped. Katie slowly withdrew the bottle, sensing that she might be full. The baby gazed up at her with sleepy eyes and smiled.

The fond, trusting smile melted Katie's heart. "You're safe now, little baby," she whispered, stroking the baby's feathery head. "I'll make sure you're safe."